STAR WARS®

JEDI APPRENTICE

The Evil Experiment

Jude Watson

SCHOLASTIC INC.

New York Toronto London Auckland Sydney
Mexico City New Delhi Hong Kong

No part of this publication may be reproduced in whole or in part, or stored in a retrieval system or transmitted in any form or by any means, electronic, mechanical, photocopying, recording, or otherwise, without written permission of the publisher. For information regarding permission, write to Scholastic Inc., Attention: Permissions Department, 555 Broadway, New York, NY 10012.

0-439-13931-7

SCHOLASTIC and associated logos are trademarks and/or registered trademarks of Scholastic Inc.

12 11 10 9 8 7 6 5 4 3 2 1   1 2 3 4 5 6/0

Printed in the U.S.A.
First Scholastic printing, February 2001

THE EVIL
EXPERIMENT

CHAPTER 1

He heard sound, but it was only a rush of white noise. His eyes were open, but he could only see vapor. He was wet, but he was not in water. Since he was not able to trust his sight or hearing, Qui-Gon Jinn decided to focus on the pain.

He tracked its location and measured its quality. It was on the left side of his chest, above his heart, and ran up to his shoulder. It wasn't a white-hot pain, but a steady burning ache, as deep as muscle and bone.

It told him he was alive.

He tried to move his right arm. The slight contraction of muscle, the effort required, seemed enormous. He hit something smooth with his fingers. He followed it slowly, tracing it up, then down. He moved his other arm and reached out his hand. Again, he met a solid wall. It was all around him. He realized that he was trapped.

A jolt of panic raced through him as he realized that he did not remember why he was here. Qui-Gon allowed it to exist and then watched it go. He breathed deeply. He was a Jedi Knight. His lightsaber was gone as well as his utility belt, but he still had the Force.

He was not alone.

As he breathed, Qui-Gon brought his mind to stillness. He told himself that his memory would return. He would not strain for it. He did not need it to live in the present moment.

He concentrated on his surroundings. Slowly he realized that he was in a transparent chamber. The reason he felt dizzy and strange was that he hung suspended, upside down. A cloudy gas surrounded him. Somehow it kept him floating in the tank. He could not see clearly through the vapor to the outside. He shifted, hoping to change position, and pain shot down his shoulder to his side. Blaster wounds were tricky. You thought the flesh was knitting, and then your wound told you otherwise if you tried too much, too soon . . .

Blaster wound.

Memories flooded back.

He had been on a mountainside with his Padawan, Obi-Wan Kenobi. They were trying to protect his friend Didi Oddo and Didi's daughter, Astri. The bounty hunter had shot Didi, and he had fallen —

Didi!

— and Obi-Wan had leaped an astonishing distance to knock the bounty hunter down. The bounty hunter had tried one last desperate maneuver, throwing a knife at Astri. His Padawan had caught it in midair. Qui-Gon remembered the pride he felt when he saw the skill of his Padawan, how Obi-Wan had timed his move and called on the Force in order to catch the deadly spinning weapon by the hilt, not the blade.

The bounty hunter had known she was defeated then. She had activated a cable line, which launched her down the mountain toward her craft. Qui-Gon had followed. He had just made it onto the launching ramp when she shot him. He remembered his surprise at the white heat in his chest, remembered falling forward into the ship and the ramp closing after him. He thought he could still hear Obi-Wan's cry.

He had left his Padawan on a remote planet with a wounded Didi — *let him be wounded, not dead* — and a young girl.

Qui-Gon moved again, and his wound screamed fire.

A female voice suddenly came to him, amplified within the tank.

"You might be experiencing some pain. It's from the chest wound. It has been treated. You will survive."

"Who are you?" Qui-Gon asked.

"You are a subject of scientific experimentation," the voice went on pleasantly. "You will not be hurt, only studied."

"What do you mean, I won't be hurt? I'm confined!" Qui-Gon protested.

"You will be treated well."

"I am here against my will! Who are you? Where am I?"

The voice did not answer. Instead, an apparatus shot into the chamber. At the end was a syringe. Qui-Gon tried to twist away, but he had nowhere to move. A needle pricked him in the neck. He watched his blood move down the transparent tube. The syringe retracted. Slowly, his body revolved until he was right-side up again.

Dizziness swamped him, but he knew it would pass. He gathered his strength, waiting out the spell.

As soon as he felt strong, he gritted his teeth against the pain and lashed out with both feet. He could not get enough leverage, and he bounced off the transparent material. He struck out with a balled fist, but got no response. The material did not bend. It did not even move a millimeter.

"Now, is that suitable behavior?" the voice chided. "You are not a child."

"I am a Jedi Knight!" Qui-Gon shouted.

"Precisely. And your life is one of service. Isn't that so?" The voice did not wait for him to respond. "Now you will be of service to the galaxy. Much more so than when you dash from world to world, waving that lightsaber around. I'm doing you a favor. You get to truly prove your commitment — how many Jedi can say the same? So relax. Let's see some of that famous Jedi meditation."

The note of dry amusement was suddenly familiar to Qui-Gon. Of course! As his memory returned, so did his suspicions.

His captor was Jenna Zan Arbor.

The brilliant scientist who appeared so perfect on the surface. The researcher who had saved whole populations from famine and plague. Yet somehow he had suspected that she was behind the plot to kill Didi. He was glad to see that his instincts had been correct.

Unfortunately, he was now her prisoner.

And he had not confided his suspicions to Obi-Wan. The boy would not know where to look, whom to suspect.

"Jenna Zan Arbor, you will not be able to hide from the Jedi," he said, matching her coolness with his own.

"Ah, so you know who I am. I'm impressed. What a specimen! It merely proves my choice is correct. I have researched you, Qui-Gon Jinn. I have found that you are an esteemed Jedi Knight, strong in the Force. You are perfect for my needs."

"And what are your needs?" Qui-Gon asked.

He heard her dry, humorless laugh. "All in good time, Qui-Gon. Just say good-bye to the life you knew. You are mine now."

CHAPTER 2

Obi-Wan Kenobi stared at the floor. It was a change. For hours, he had been staring at the wall.

He was in the Jedi Temple med center. With one look, Obi-Wan knew Didi needed the best care in the galaxy. He and Astri had brought Didi in, talking to him constantly during the journey, even though he had long ago lapsed into unconsciousness.

The Jedi medics and healers had rushed Didi into an interior room. They had only come out to tell Obi-Wan and Astri that Didi was still alive, and that they were hopeful.

Over the long night, Bant had sat by his side, then Garen, his best friends at the Temple. Bant did not speak, but occasionally would slip her slender hand into his. All night they had sat, waiting for news. At last he had sent his friends away to eat breakfast. He could not eat. He could not sleep.

Didi struggled for life in the next room. What about Qui-Gon? Was his Master alive or dead?

He is alive, Obi-Wan told himself fiercely. *He is alive because he must be alive.*

He had seen the blaster fire hit Qui-Gon in the chest near the heart. He had seen him stagger and fall back. But Qui-Gon had reserves of strength that were astonishing. Even if he were the bounty hunter's captive, he would manage to stay alive until Obi-Wan could find him. The bounty hunter would not leave him to die.

He told himself this, over and over. But when he remembered her impassive face, her ruthlessness in battle, Obi-Wan felt despair.

And still I sit here. Waiting.

He had briefed Yoda and Tahl, the Jedi Knight who was coordinating the search for Qui-Gon. He had told them everything he knew. But he could not tell them where the bounty hunter was headed. They did not know who had hired her to track down Didi. They did not know why. They did not even know her name. There were too many questions. And Qui-Gon's life hung in the balance.

Yoda had assigned several Jedi teams to investigate Qui-Gon's disappearance. Tahl was trying to crack the code of Jenna Zan Arbor's datapad, as well as look for clues that might lead to the identity and whereabouts of the mysterious bounty hunter. Everything that could possibly be done was being done. All the resources of the Jedi were turned toward finding Qui-Gon. Except for Obi-Wan. He could only sit.

"Have you memorized the floor yet?"

Astri's voice broke into his thoughts. She gave him a half smile. "I have. There are twenty-seven squares of stone between here and the wall."

"It can't be much longer," Obi-Wan said.

She sighed and leaned forward on her knees, clasping her hands together. Astri was tall and slender, with midnight-black hair that hung in curls to the middle of her back. She was older than Obi-Wan and had run Didi's Café with her father. He did not know Astri well, but he had come to know that she did not like to show weakness or affection. Having her father shot before her eyes had devastated her. Trying to conceal her shock and despair was defeating her.

"I never knew my birth parents," Astri said as she stared down at the floor. "Someone left me in Didi's Café. He took me in."

"I didn't know that," Obi-Wan said.

"I think whoever left me there must have cared about me somewhat," Astri went on softly. "They chose Didi to be my father. They knew he wouldn't give me away to be placed by the government. They knew his heart would melt at the sight of a baby. And it did. I was lucky."

"Yes, I can see that," Obi-Wan said. "Sometimes the home you find is the one you are meant to have." It was how he felt about the Temple. And Qui-Gon.

She turned to look at him, sorrow in her dark eyes. "I'm sure Qui-Gon will be all right. He's so strong. I've known him all my life, Obi-Wan. I have seen how strong he is."

Obi-Wan nodded. If Qui-Gon were dead, he would know it. He would feel it.

"I know you want to find him. Thank you for staying here with me."

"I wouldn't know where to start," Obi-Wan confessed. "We don't know why the bounty hunter was hired."

"We know she tried to steal that datapad," Astri said. "So we know there is information on it that is valuable to someone. And we know that datapad belonged to Jenna Zan Arbor. Fligh stole it from her."

"But he also stole Senator S'orn's datapad," Obi-Wan pointed out. "So the connection to the bounty hunter could lie there. Your friend Fligh is dead and cannot give us answers. And even if we did find out who hired the bounty hunter, we still don't know where she would take Qui-Gon."

Astri nodded. "But you will find him," she said. "The Jedi can do anything."

She stood, wincing as she did so. Astri had a wrenched shoulder, as well as bumps and bruises from being dragged down the mountainside, a prisoner of the bounty hunter's whip.

"Are you all right?" Obi-Wan asked. "The medic could give you something for the pain."

"No, I want to stay alert. What about you?" Astri asked Obi-Wan. "How is your leg?"

Obi-Wan felt the bandage on his thigh. His leg had been sliced by the spiking of the bounty hunter's whip. The wound had been bathed in a bacta tank. It would heal. Already the pain was ebbing.

And Qui-Gon? Have his wounds been attended to?

Astri prowled around the small waiting room. It was designed for comfort and calm, in colors of pale blue and white. The seating areas were grouped for both privacy and intimacy.

Astri looked out at the view of Coruscant. "I am so grateful to the Jedi. The healers and medics have been so good. I just wish they were *faster*."

The door to the inner treatment rooms opened. The Jedi healer, Winna Di Yuni, came toward them, dressed in the light blue tunic of a medic. Obi-Wan had been glad when Winna had taken over Didi's care. She was an elder Jedi, tall and strong, with a gentle manner. She was renowned for her great skill as a diagnostician. She had a vast knowledge of all the diseases in the galaxy.

Now Obi-Wan's heart beat faster when he saw the look on Winna's face. He knew in a sudden flash that she was not bringing good news. He stood, and Astri quickly crossed to his side.

Winna looked at Astri kindly and gestured for them to take a seat. She sat opposite them. "We have done all we can for your father," she said. "It is up to Didi now. His life energy is very low. He himself must find the strength to fight."

Obi-Wan saw Astri swallow. "His wounds are bad?" he asked.

Winna nodded. "Very bad, I'm afraid. But that is not the only problem. Infection has set in, an infection that we cannot identify. We are searching all our data banks. I did not want to come out here until we found out what infection this is, but you need to know what is happening."

"I don't understand," Astri said. "You are the best healers in the galaxy. If you don't know what is wrong with Didi, who will know?"

"We do not know everything," Winna said

gently. "The galaxy is a very large place. Infections and diseases pop up everywhere, new ones all the time. I have no doubt that we will locate the source of this one. But it may take time."

"Didi doesn't *have* time," Astri said, gripping her hands together. "That is what you mean."

"Do not look for the worst thing," Winna said. "Think of the best thing. We will identify this infection and treat it."

Astri bit her lip. "Can I see him?"

"Yes, of course. He is not conscious. But he might feel your presence. Come with me."

Astri followed Winna. She looked as though she were sleepwalking. Obi-Wan felt stunned as well. Didi was larger than life. He had expected the healers to come out with good news any second.

Instead, there was only more waiting . . .

The door to the main hallway opened. Tahl walked in with Yoda at her side.

"How is Didi?" Yoda asked. "Heard we did that news there is."

"He has an infection that they cannot identify," Obi-Wan said. "Winna tried to reassure Astri, but I can see that she is worried."

"Do her best, she will. A great amount, that is." Yoda pressed a button and one of the seating cushions lowered. They were adjustable for the many species in the Jedi Temple. He lowered himself onto the cushion, then leaned on his staff. "And you, Obi-Wan? No sleep you've had, I fear."

"I can't sleep until I know Qui-Gon is safe," Obi-Wan said. "Is there any news?"

Tahl's sightless green-and-gold striped eyes were filled with frustration. She shook her head, her lips tightening. "I've got every contact working, Obi-Wan," she told him. "Giett has returned from his long mission and is back on the Council, so Ki-Adi-Mundi is helping with the galactic search. We could not ask for a better analyst."

Obi-Wan nodded. Ki-Adi-Mundi had stood in for Giett on the Jedi Council for a time. With his binary brain, he was able to sift through an extraordinary amount of information and analyze it.

"We don't have anything on the bounty hunter," Tahl continued. "She has no known friends or comrades. Those who have hired her refuse to talk, even to us. They're scared of retaliation. But we're working on it."

"What about Jenna Zan Arbor's datapad?" Obi-Wan asked. "There must be something on it that somebody wants."

"We can't crack the code," Tahl said. "Most scientists encode their data — it doesn't mean that she is connected to the bounty hunter or

Qui-Gon's disappearance. But just in case, we don't want to alert her that we're on her trail. We have to explore all options until we find the right way to proceed. I won't rest until we find him, Obi-Wan."

"I know," Obi-Wan told her. Tahl was just as close to Qui-Gon. They had gone through Temple training together.

"Teams we have all over the Duneeden system, Obi-Wan," Yoda told him. "Find we will a trace of the bounty hunter's ship."

"We know the ship was equipped with a hyperdrive," Tahl said worriedly. "There's a good chance she didn't remain in the Duneeden system at all. But we're going to check out every lead."

"News I have of one Jedi team," Yoda told them. "Dispatched they were to Zan Arbor's lab on her home planet of Ventrux. Find we did that the lab has been closed down. Dismissed the workers were, and paid off."

A spark lit Tahl's eyes. "Well, at least that's something. Jenna Zan Arbor has to be involved. We've got to crack that code!"

Yoda nodded. "Think we do that she has another base of operations," he said. "Searching for it, we are." He turned to Obi-Wan. "A difficult time for calm it is. Yet calm you must find. When news comes, go with a steady heart you must. Direction you need. Direction we will find."

Obi-Wan's heart was far from steady. But Yoda was right. He must be resolute, and resolution only came with calm.

The door to the inner chamber slid open. Winna came forward quickly.

"Didi's infection has been identified. The blaster fire must have been tainted with a solution to trigger infection."

"Do you have a cure?" Obi-Wan asked.

Winna nodded. "The treatment has been discovered. It is an antitoxin. But I have bad news. The lab that sells it has been shut down. There are no stockpiles that we can find. This lab was the only source in the galaxy."

Obi-Wan glanced at Tahl. By the look on her face, he knew she was thinking the same thing. Yoda nodded slowly.

"What's the name of the lab?" Obi-Wan asked.

"Arbor Industries," Winna replied.

It was the answer Obi-Wan had expected to hear.

CHAPTER 3

He was getting weaker, not stronger. Qui-Gon felt his body float. He wanted to give himself up to the sensation, bob in the oddly pleasant vapor, let it lull him into long sleeps. Even in his worst illness, he had never felt so weak.

Was she doing something to keep him weak? Blood was extracted regularly, but that still did not account for his fatigue.

Isolated from the world, from other living creatures, he knew the Force still worked around him. He closed his eyes and reached out to it. He would gather it around him like a shield. Qui-Gon felt the Force move inside the chamber. He concentrated harder . . .

Through the veil of vapor, indicator lights outside his chamber glowed. Dimly, he heard a sensor ring shrilly and the sound of hurrying footsteps. Then Zan Arbor's amplified voice again:

"You just accessed the Force. Good. Don't be afraid to do so."

"How did you know?" Qui-Gon asked. The question was out of his mouth before he had a chance to think. His surprise had triggered it.

"I am monitoring your body functions. When you access the Force, your body temperature drops. Your heartbeat slows. So strange. Once I thought the Force would have the opposite effect. But it works mysteriously. That's why it is so interesting to study."

So she was studying the Force. Qui-Gon turned this new fact over in his mind. The Force could not be measured or manufactured. But if a scientist of Jenna Zan Arbor's brilliance was studying it, it was possible she could discover things she should not know. He must not underestimate her intelligence.

Which meant he could not use the Force to heal himself.

"Why are you so interested in the Force?" he asked.

"Ah, we are full of questions today," she murmured.

"There is not much else to do in here," Qui-Gon pointed out.

"What about your famous Jedi meditation? That should pass the time."

"Even meditation has its limits," Qui-Gon said dryly.

He heard a low laugh. "Why shouldn't I study the Force? Why should the Jedi be the only ones to study it?"

Qui-Gon thought before answering. He needed to keep her talking. He needed to appear to be interested in her studies.

"That is a good point," he said. "We believe the Force connects us all."

"That is exactly my point!" Zan Arbor said excitedly. "The Jedi should welcome my interest."

"How do you know they do not?" Qui-Gon asked. "You haven't asked us."

"I don't need your permission," she snapped.

He was losing her. "I didn't mean that," he said. "You are a brilliant researcher. You might want to share your findings with the galaxy."

"When I am ready," she said. "But not until then."

"And what are you looking for?"

She did not answer for a moment, and he was afraid the conversation was over. Then she said, "My colleagues are fools."

Qui-Gon waited. He did not want to seem too eager. Something told him that Jenna Zan Arbor wanted to talk.

"You've traveled. You must have seen that the galaxy is full of fools."

"I have seen that many beings do not trust their eyes, their minds, or their hearts," Qui-Gon said.

"Exactly! So you see what I have to deal with," Jenna Zan Arbor said, her voice warming. "I have just come from a conference at the Senate. My colleagues are chasing dreams, not ideas. New ways to make starships go faster. New engines, new fuels, new hyperdrives. They try to find ways to make weapons more powerful, more effective. They look for new sources of power. Faster. Bigger. Better. That is what they chase. They ignore the most powerful energy in the galaxy. The Force is far more important than any of these. With the Force, you can move *minds.* That is much more important than ships!"

"I would agree with that," Qui-Gon said.

"How ironic," Zan Arbor said. "Only a Jedi would understand. And yet only the Jedi can be my best subjects. The others . . . even those who had the Force, who were, as you call them, Force-sensitive . . . they did not know what they had. They could not control it. It is hard to measure something that will not be controlled. That was the flaw in my experiments."

Qui-Gon had a sudden notion that chilled him. Was Zan Arbor keeping him in a condition of weakness so that he would use the Force to heal himself?

He could do nothing in this chamber. He would never escape if he didn't get out, even for a short time.

Perhaps he could form some sort of bond with his captor.

"I will make a deal with you," he said.

"I hardly think you are in a position to offer deals," Jenna Zan Arbor said, amused.

"I think I am," Qui-Gon returned quietly. "I have something you want. That puts me exactly in that position."

There was a pause. "What do you want?"

"I want to be let out of this chamber for two hours a day," Qui-Gon said. "If you do this, I will use the Force to heal myself. If you do not, I will not access it."

"You will die," she warned.

"Yes," Qui-Gon replied calmly. "As a Jedi, I am prepared for death. It does not frighten me."

"I do not make deals!" Zan Arbor cried shrilly. "*I* am the leader here! *I* make the decisions!"

He did not answer. He closed his eyes. He was gambling that she would not refuse him. He sensed the fever in her, the compulsion to follow through on her experiments. She would give in.

"All right," she snapped. "But not two hours. One hour. That's all. Do we have a deal?"

"We have a deal," Qui-Gon answered. He had expected her to counter with one hour. It was not a problem. One hour would have to be enough.

CHAPTER 4

Yoda, Tahl, and Obi-Wan were silent for a long moment. The news that Jenna Zan Arbor controlled access to Didi's antitoxin disturbed them.

"It's very strange," Winna continued. "Not only is Arbor Industries closed, but there is no other source we can find anywhere. There must be some mistake, something we haven't thought to check. This infection is very rare, but still, Arbor Industries should have allowed other labs to stock the antitoxin. This is an astonishing breach of ethics. They left no word when they'll reopen, or where —"

"Something you should know, there is," Yoda interrupted. "Under suspicion by the Jedi, Jenna Zan Arbor is."

"She could be involved in Qui-Gon Jinn's disappearance," Tahl said.

"Not to mention murder," Obi-Wan added.

Winna's frown grew deeper as shock slowly registered on her face. "You mean that Zan Arbor has *deliberately* deprived the galaxy of her medicines?"

"I think it a very great possibility," Tahl said.

Winna's expression was grim. "My patient will die without that antitoxin."

"I don't understand." Astri had come up behind them so quietly they had not heard her. "You say that Jenna Zan Arbor has the medicine that my father needs, and you can't find her?"

"I am afraid that is the case," Winna said.

Obi-Wan went to Astri. He hovered by her side, uncertain of what to say or do. "You mustn't lose hope," he said.

She nodded, her mouth tightening. He saw her shoulders shaking. She was trying not to cry aloud.

"Obi-Wan is right," Winna said. "The antitoxin must be held somewhere in the galaxy. We will find it, Astri."

"I know you will do everything you can."

"Our good friend Didi is, Astri," Yoda told her. "Take good care of him, we will."

"You are very kind." Astri turned and walked toward the window. She stared out blankly.

"She has lost hope," Tahl murmured.

"Bad news, it was," Yoda said. "Hard to absorb."

"I'd better get back," Winna said tersely, and hurried off.

"Go to Astri, you should," Yoda told Obi-Wan. "Her friend you are. Console her, you must. Hope must not die while Didi lives."

But Astri wasn't really his friend. He'd just met her. And he wasn't very good at consolation. If only Qui-Gon were here!

Yoda and Tahl left, and Obi-Wan went to stand awkwardly by Astri's side.

"He's going to die," she said. "And I will be alone."

"We cannot lose hope," Obi-Wan said. "The Jedi are capable of extraordinary things. We will find the antitoxin or Jenna Zan Arbor."

"I am certain that you will," Astri said. "But will Didi still be alive? He looks so small, Obi-Wan. His spirit filled him. Now he's so weak . . ."

"He is not weak," Obi-Wan said. "He had one of the strongest spirits I've ever seen. It is still there, his strength."

"I thought I had troubles once," Astri said slowly. "Running a business wasn't easy. But now I know despair for the first time. Even if Didi survives, we have lost everything. The café has been closed by our landlord. We owe him credits we cannot pay. Even as I sit by Didi's bedside, begging him to live, I wonder what he will return to. And it's my fault. I spent all our savings on improvements for the café. We have nothing."

Obi-Wan did not have to wonder what Qui-Gon would say. "You have each other."

"You're right, Obi-Wan. I'm feeling sorry for myself." Astri rubbed her forehead. "It's just that I'm so tired."

"Why don't you rest here?" Obi-Wan suggested, indicating the seating area. "You wouldn't have to go to the sleeping quarters. I will make sure you won't be disturbed, unless . . . unless Didi awakens."

Astri sank onto the cushions and laid her head down. "Maybe just an hour," she said as her eyes closed.

Obi-Wan decided he would stay until he was sure she was asleep. His nerves were jumping. He was anxious to check with Tahl and the Jedi code breakers. He wanted to be present when they cracked the datapad.

He reached into his tunic to remove the Force-sensitive river stone that Qui-Gon had given him. He often found comfort in turning the smooth stone around in his hand. It made him feel closer to Qui-Gon.

A crackle alerted him that there was something else in his inner pocket. Obi-Wan took it out. It was a durasheet. On it, Jenna Zan Arbor had written the names of the guests she had invited to Didi's Café. The names were already beginning to fade.

Obi-Wan thought back to only a few days before. Qui-Gon had asked her to write out the information when they'd visited her at her hotel.

Qui-Gon never did anything without a reason. Obi-Wan frowned, thinking hard. They had gone to see Zan Arbor because they had discovered that she had learned about Didi's Café from Didi's friend Fligh. Fligh had stolen the datapad of both Senator S'orn and Zan Arbor. Later he had been found dead, his body drained of blood. At that point, they did not know if Zan Arbor was involved. They were just following a thread.

In other words, Zan Arbor hadn't been a suspect. So why had Qui-Gon asked for this list?

Back then, Obi-Wan thought that the Outlaw Tech gang had hired the bounty hunter. But Qui-Gon must have had his doubts. Had he been trying to link the bounty hunter to Zan Arbor?

They had never solved the mystery of how the bounty hunter had been able to break into Didi's Café after Zan Arbor's guests had left. They knew the café had been locked up tight, every door and window bolted.

Could Qui-Gon have wondered if one of the guests had stayed behind? Astri might not have noticed in the confusion of departure.

And the bounty hunter was a master of disguise . . .

Obi-Wan looked over at Astri. She was sleeping peacefully. He could leave her for a short time.

He crossed to a small desk in the corner. Quickly, he copied the fading names onto a fresh durasheet and tossed the old one in the trash container.

He headed out the door. It wasn't much to go on, but it was a direction.

CHAPTER 5

Yamele Polidor
Nontal Quincu
Aleck W'a Ni Odus
Dobei Eranusite
B'Zun Mai
Reesa On
Von Taub

Obi-Wan took an air taxi to the Official Committee Liaison Office at the Senate. This office handled the transportation and residence needs of the many committees from around the galaxy that came to petition the Senate. Since it was a Jedi request, he was given the homeworlds and contact information of each being on the list.

Quickly, Obi-Wan scanned it. Only three of the guests were still staying on Coruscant. The others had returned to their homeworlds. He would start here. If he found nothing, he would move on. If he had to travel to the Outer Rim for a clue, he would do it.

Yamele Polidor and Von Taub still had business with the Senate and were staying in a guesthouse nearby. Obi-Wan went there first. He found them together in the sitting room, going over the record of the meeting they had attended that day.

Obi-Wan explained that he was on a Jedi mission to discover who had broken into Didi's Café after their group had left.

Yamele Polidor was a petite Rindian with pointed ears and two eight-fingered hands. She nodded politely at Obi-Wan. "Of course I will be glad to help."

The Corweillian Von Taub nodded. "As will I."

"Did anyone come into the café while you were there?" Obi-Wan asked.

"Just the members of our own party," Yamele Polidor answered in the low, singsong manner of a Rindian.

"Did you notice anyone on the street outside?"

Von Taub shook his head. "We left, and the owner of the café, a young woman, locked the door after us. Jenna Zan Arbor was very upset with the service and food. I didn't think it was that bad, myself." He smiled. "Maybe I'm more used to disorganization. But Jenna is a scientist who can't tolerate disorder."

"Do you know the other names on this list well?" Obi-Wan asked. He handed the list to them.

Yamele Polidor ran one of her long fingers down the list. "I know all of these scientists personally, except for Dobei Eranusite and Reesa On."

"I know Dobei quite well," Von Taub said. "Reesa On was a stranger to me as well."

"Did anyone know her?" Obi-Wan asked.

"Jenna Zan Arbor," Yamele Polidor answered.

"Yes, they worked on a research project together," Von Taub added. "Jenna was very complimentary about her skills as a scientist. None of the rest of us knew her."

Obi-Wan kept his voice steady despite his rising excitement. "Do you remember what she looked like?"

"Not really," Yamele Polidor said with a shrug. "Tall, maybe? She was humanoid. That, I remember."

"Very striking," Von Taub said. "She wore a silk turban and a lovely septsilk robe."

Obi-Wan realized he had seen her himself. He had a vague memory of a woman in a jeweled turban. He pushed his urgency away and left his mind open, let the memory come as it would, as he had been taught. The information he sought would come to him.

He and Qui-Gon had been talking to Astri when the guests arrived. He remembered the look of distaste on Jenna Zan Arbor's face. And one tall woman had gathered her rich robe around her as if it would get dirty from touching a chair or the floor. She had very strong hands . . .

It had been her. The bounty hunter.

He was sure of it. And now he had a name.

"One last question," Obi-Wan said. "Do you know if Zan Arbor has more than one lab? I know that her main lab is on Ventrux."

Both the scientists looked puzzled. "But why would she need another lab?" Von Taub asked.

"I have never heard such a thing," Yamele Polidor added.

"Thank you for your help," he said, rising and bowing. He hurried outside and immediately summoned Tahl on his comlink.

"We could have a lead," he said. "I think the bounty hunter posed as a scientist named Reesa On. Most likely she disguised herself in order to steal the datapad back from Didi and Astri. She would have if Qui-Gon and I hadn't returned and surprised her. The Senate still lists her as being on Coruscant. She's supposed to inform them when she returns to her home-world. I have the address."

"Don't go alone," Tahl warned. "Wait, and I'll send a team to you."

"I can't wait," Obi-Wan argued. "She's listed at a lodging only a short distance from here. Let me at least see if she's there."

"Do not engage her in battle or even show yourself," Tahl warned. "She could lead us to Qui-Gon."

"I won't," Obi-Wan promised. "I'll just keep her under surveillance."

"I'll see what I can discover from here," Tahl told him. "Good work, Obi-Wan."

Obi-Wan cut the communication and headed down the walkway that led to Vertex, the street that was listed as Reesa On's address. He drew his robe around him and lifted his hood to cover his face. He must follow Tahl's advice. He knew Tahl was just as anxious as he was to find Qui-Gon. If she urged caution, it was only because being careful would bring them to Qui-Gon faster.

The inn where Reesa On was staying was similar to the one he had left. Many small guest-houses existed around the Senate to cater to wealthy guests with Senate business that required long stays. It was a far cry from the shabby, decrepit inn where he'd had his first confrontation with the bounty hunter.

And it had security. Guests used swipe cards to enter. All others had to be announced.

He loitered outside the building, wondering what to do. Most likely he would not be lucky enough to see her enter or leave. And would he recognize her even if she did? She had impersonated an old man, a wealthy scientist, and a young boy parking speeders at a grand hotel. Her powers of transformation were incredible.

The door to the house slid open, and someone stood on the threshold. Concealed behind a row of speeders, Obi-Wan looked carefully. A Rodian stood for a moment as if to test the weather. Even a master of disguise could not impersonate a Rodian. This one was bulky and short, with green skin and the usual ridge of spines along his skull. No, this was not the bounty hunter.

Quickly, Obi-Wan stood and crossed the walkway. He headed up the ramp and nodded at the Rodian, then walked through the open door. It slid shut behind him.

The guesthouse was operated by automation. He glanced around quickly at the terminals set in the walls. Here guests used their cards to pick up messages. He spied a keyboard and quickly typed in *Reesa On.*

ROOM 1289

Obi-Wan took the turbolift to the twelfth floor. He moved quickly down the hall and stood in front of Room 1289. He pressed his ear to the door, every sense alert. Listening was a Jedi skill that was honed in exercises during Temple training.

He heard the soft whisper of fabric. Its regular movement told him that it was just a curtain stirring with a breeze. He could not hear footsteps or even breathing.

What now? Obi-Wan knew that it would not be the last time he would ask himself that question. Without Qui-Gon, he was unsure of every step.

Obi-Wan was concentrating so hard on the sounds behind the door that he heard the opening of the turbolift just a second too late. He felt a surge in the Force, warning him an instant before blaster fire slammed into the door over his head.

CHAPTER 6

Obi-Wan ducked and rolled, reaching for his lightsaber at the same time. It was activated and ready for the next round of fire even as he leaped in the air toward his assailant.

"Obi-Wan, no!" Astri screamed.

She fell backward, the blaster flying from her grasp. Her feet flew up, barely missing the blade of the lightsaber. Obi-Wan quickly deactivated it. She landed with a *thump* and a cry that must have been heard by every guest on the floor.

"What are you doing here?" he hissed.

"What are you doing here?" she shouted at the same time.

Obi-Wan silenced her with a gesture and pointed to Reesa On's door. Astri stood, straightening her tunic.

"She's not there. I already checked the room."

"What?"

Down the hallway, a door slid open a few centimeters, and two orange eyes peered out at them.

"Come on," Obi-Wan muttered. "We can't talk here."

He grabbed Astri's blaster and tucked it into his utility belt. He didn't speak while they were in the turbolift. Astri stole a few glances at him. She opened her mouth once or twice, but decided to stay silent.

He waited until they had left the guesthouse and had walked a short distance from it. He struggled to gather his patience. He did not want to show his anger. But he did not have Qui-Gon's gift for serenity.

"What were you doing there?" he demanded. "You could have ruined everything!"

"I thought you would need help —"

"You're a cook, not a Jedi!" Obi-Wan burst out. "How did you find me, anyway? Did you follow me?"

"I read that durasheet you left," Astri said. "I recognized the names. They were the guests at Jenna's dinner party at our café. And you think the bounty hunter was one of them."

Obi-Wan stared at her in disbelief. "So how did you find out where Reesa On was staying? And how did you find out that the bounty hunter *is* Reesa On? Did you go to the Senate Liaison Office, too? That could tip her off!"

Astri waved her hand. "I don't have to go through official channels. I'm Didi's daughter, remember? Everyone who comes to the Senate doesn't just go through a security check. They go through a *criminal* check."

"You mean they're scanned for outstanding warrants?" Obi-Wan asked.

She grinned as she sidestepped a group of tourists. "No, they're checked out *by* criminals. Nanno L'a and his gang keep tabs on all Senate petitioners and commission members who visit from other worlds. You never know who might have something worth stealing. So I talked to Nanno. He'd do anything for Didi. He gave me the rundown on the names on the list. His gang had copies of the textdocs on each of them. The only one who came up blank was Reesa On. She had a couple of ID facts in her textdoc, but no record of financial transactions. For someone with plenty of wealth, that seemed odd. So I figured Reesa On was a false identity. Nanno knew where Reesa On was staying. So I went there."

"How do you know she wasn't in her room?" Obi-Wan asked. He felt a little irritated that Astri was able to focus on Reesa On quicker than he had.

"These guesthouses all use the nearby cafés and restaurants for food service," Astri explained. "I went to the Galaxy Grill down the street and asked my friend Endami for the service code. Then I pretended to have a meal delivery and punched in the code." She shrugged. "That got me inside. The service code will also tell you who is staying in what room. It was easy."

Easy! "So did you break into her room?" Obi-Wan asked irritably.

"I knocked and said I had a food delivery," Astri said. "No one answered, so I opened the door."

"But it was locked."

Astri smiled. "I learned how to bypass a basic security lock when I was seven, Obi-Wan. My guess is she's not coming back. There was a travel bag there, but it's filled with things that are supposed to make you *think* someone is there."

"If that makes sense, I'd sure like to hear why," Obi-Wan grumbled.

"It's got a new personal care kit with soap and bath items, but they haven't been used. A couple of fresh tunics and sleepwear that haven't been worn. My guess is that the bounty hunter never even stayed there at all — she just paid up for her two week minimum so that she'd have an official address."

Astri was probably right, Obi-Wan thought.

They were no closer to finding Reesa On's true identity. In frustration, he turned away and started to walk.

"Where are we going?" Astri asked.

"*You* are going back to the Temple," Obi-Wan said. "I'm trying to find Qui-Gon. This is Jedi business."

"This is *my* business." Astri stopped short, forcing Obi-Wan to stop, too. "Didi isn't waking up, Obi-Wan," she said, her dark eyes serious. "Not without that antitoxin. You and I both know that. And Reesa On is our first clue to where Jenna Zan Arbor is. You think she is holding Qui-Gon, right?"

Obi-Wan nodded reluctantly.

"So I have just as much reason to find Reesa On as you do. The bounty hunter could lead us to Zan Arbor. And I have another reason. Nanno told me that because of Fligh's murder and Qui-Gon's disappearance, a warrant has been issued for the bounty hunter's arrest by the Coruscant security forces. There's a reward, too. Don't you see?" Astri tossed the curls out of her eyes impatiently. "This is the only thing I can do for Didi. I can find the antitoxin *and* get us a new stake. All I have to do is find Reesa On."

He shook his head. "It's too dangerous."

"I can help you, Obi-Wan."

"What are you going to do, cook us out of danger?" Obi-Wan asked skeptically.

"There are other things I can do!" Astri protested. "Do I have to point out that I found Reesa On quicker than you did? You have to admit I have *some* skills."

"Not with a blaster," Obi-Wan muttered. He thought for a moment. He knew Astri well enough to guess that if he didn't include her, she would try to find the bounty hunter on her own. She would be safer with him.

"We can team up, but I need a couple of conditions," he said. "First of all, you don't use a blaster."

"But I need protection," Astri protested. "And I'm getting better at aiming."

Obi-Wan winced. "Sure. You came within *five* centimeters of killing me instead of six. I'll make a deal with you. We have to wait until Tahl comes up with information about Reesa On. I'll go back to the Temple with you and choose a new weapon. We'll see how you do with a vibroblade. You should have some kind of protection, I suppose."

"What's the other condition?" Astri asked.

"If things get dangerous, I'm going to ask you to return to the Temple," Obi-Wan said. "A pile of credits isn't going to help Didi if you're dead."

Astri hesitated.

"I know you think I have no right to tell you what to do," Obi-Wan said. "That's true. But I represent the Jedi. You must trust *us,* not just me."

Reluctantly, Astri nodded. "So we're a team?"

Obi-Wan nodded grimly. "For now."

Astri was hopeless with a blaster, but she was adept with a vibroblade. Obi-Wan gave her a quick lesson in strategy and defense. Her body was agile and strong, and she was surprisingly quick.

"Try to stay behind me or at my side," Obi-Wan told her. "But don't get in the way of my lightsaber."

"Don't worry," Astri told him.

The door to the training room opened and Tahl hurried inside. She immediately turned her face toward Didi's daughter.

"Astri, you're here, too?"

"Yes."

"I have a clue," she said. "It's not much, but it's something. I couldn't find anything on Reesa On, but just on a hunch I ran the name through the language of Sorrus."

"The bounty hunter's home planet," Obi-Wan told Astri.

"It turns out that 'reesa on' means something in an obscure Sorrusian dialect," Tahl said. "It's spoken by a tribe living in a remote area of Sorrus."

"What does it mean?" Astri asked.

Tahl's mouth twisted. "'Catch me.' There is actually a childhood game among this tribe called 'reesa on.'"

"So the name is a taunt," Obi-Wan said. "Catch me if you can."

"Exactly," Tahl agreed. "I have the coordinates of the tribe's area. I doubt that the bounty hunter is there. Jedi teams have been sent on other leads. Most are working on finding Zan Arbor's lab by tracking medical shipments. This is such a tiny lead. Still . . ."

"We could find out more about her," Obi-Wan said.

"And we have nothing else to go on," Astri agreed.

Tahl cocked her head as if testing the meaning behind Astri's words. "We?"

"I'm going with Obi-Wan," Astri declared.

Tahl shook her head. "You can't go on a Jedi mission, Astri."

"But this isn't a mission," Astri argued. "There's no danger involved."

"Where the bounty hunter is or could be, danger is there," Tahl said sharply. "Don't forget that."

Astri's chin set defiantly. Even though Tahl

couldn't see her, Tahl was able to pick up her stubbornness. She frowned.

"I promised Astri she could come with me for a time," Obi-Wan told Tahl. "The bounty hunter shot her father, Tahl. She has a right to track her, too. And she'll be in less danger if she's with me. I'll send her back to the Temple if I think the bounty hunter is on Sorrus."

"I don't like this," Tahl declared. "I should confer with Yoda. You need to be temporarily assigned to a Jedi Master, Obi-Wan. Or else stay at the Temple."

"But I'm not going on a mission, just scouting out a lead. Qui-Gon needs my help," Obi-Wan argued.

He saw the hesitancy on Tahl's face.

"I have to find my Master, Tahl," Obi-Wan said steadily. "I feel him. I know he needs me. Let me go."

"I'm sure we are breaking several rules here," Tahl murmured.

Obi-Wan smiled. "Qui-Gon would like that."

Tahl smiled, too. "Yes," she said softly. "There is a tech transport ship that could drop you off at the capital city closest to the desert tribe . . ."

Obi-Wan looked at Astri. "Let's go."

CHAPTER 7

Qui-Gon waited for his hour of freedom. He did not know when Zan Arbor would grant it. He wanted it so badly it was difficult for him to think of anything else.

Being suspended in this vapor without sight and sound was a particular kind of torture. Deprived of his senses, he experienced dislocation. He had to be conscious of his mind at all times, wrench it back to its surroundings. He could move his muscles very little, and he flexed them, one by one, every half hour. That was an effort. The constant withdrawal of blood was beginning to sap his strength.

He knew that at the Temple he was appreciated for several things: his physical strength, his connection to the living Force, and his patience. Now he hung in a chamber, and none of these things were available to him. He would just have to find other things he was good at.

The loss of his patience was the worst. He could not calm his raging desire to be free. He dreamed of freedom as another might dream of food.

So much for his great forbearance. Now he realized that he had many more lessons to learn. How many times had he heard Yoda advise an advanced student that for a Jedi, true mastery of a skill was only the beginning step to understanding it? How many times had he said the same to Obi-Wan?

The more you know, Padawan, the less you know.

By the time this was over, he would see how much he still had to learn about patience.

Was it his imagination, or was the vapor beginning to thin? Qui-Gon looked down and could see his feet. Yes, the vapor was slowly siphoning away. Did that mean that Zan Arbor was about to release him?

He had made no plans for his first release. His only intention was to talk to Zan Arbor again. Somehow he felt he would gain a clue of how to proceed.

The vapor cleared. His heartbeat quickened. He saw movement outside the transparent wall of the chamber.

"I see you're excited, Qui-Gon." Zan Arbor's

cool voice penetrated the chamber. "Try to contain yourself. I didn't throw you a party."

The chamber walls slid down, disappearing into the floor. Qui-Gon's knees buckled and he fell forward. The floor against his cheek felt like a gift. Sense had been deprived for so long that the texture of the stone, the coolness of the temperature, felt like fresh rain on his face.

He saw Zan Arbor's boots approach, centimeters from his nose.

"Men have fallen at my feet, but it was in my younger days," she remarked. "How nice to see I still have that power."

He would not speak until he knew his voice would be steady. He reached deep inside for the reserve of strength he knew was still there. He had protected that reserve during the long hours of his captivity.

He did not raise himself to his knees until he knew he would be able to get to his feet. He stood in one smooth motion. He locked his knees.

He had always seen her in rich robes, her hair elaborately styled. Now Jenna Zan Arbor was dressed simply in a white tunic and trousers. She was smaller than he remembered. Her hair was drawn back and held with an intricate silver clip.

"I would have thought you were the type of

woman who prefers beings to meet you eye to eye," he said.

She smiled. "But so few can. I am told I am intimidating."

"That's what makes the few who match you more valuable."

"I have no interest in other beings anymore, or any conventions of what the majority of those in the galaxy want," Jenna Zan Arbor said coolly. "I don't need friendship. Only my work drives me. Nil!"

A tall, thin being shuffled forward. Qui-Gon recognized a being from the planet Quint. Quints were covered in delicate fur and had small heads with triangular eyes. They were extraordinarily quick and fast. Nil had two blasters strapped to his waist. He put his sharp-nailed hands on his blasters and gave Qui-Gon a contemptuous glance.

"Watch him," Zan Arbor instructed Nil. "Even an unarmed, weakened Jedi is a formidable opponent." She turned back to Qui-Gon. "I should tell you that my security is state of the art. And if you attempt escape, Nil will not hesitate to shoot you."

Qui-Gon had no intention of attempting to escape. He knew he was too weak. He didn't acknowledge what she'd said, but ignored Nil and returned to their conversation.

"How does your work drive you?" Qui-Gon asked. While they talked, he examined the space around him without seeming to glance. It was a Jedi skill. To Zan Arbor, he appeared to be totally fixated on her face.

"How does my work drive me?" she repeated, puzzled. "That seems obvious."

Stone floor. Long metal lab tables. Records piled neatly on a desk. Sensors, computer bank, lab equipment along one wall.

"Not at all. Scientists are driven for different reasons," Qui-Gon said, beginning to stroll about to stretch his legs. Nil followed a few paces behind. "Some for pure research — they have a hunger for how things work. Some want to be remembered, to have their name on a discovery. Some think of living beings and want to help them. Which kind of scientist are you?"

Only one exit, a durasteel door. A security pad mounted to one side. He would need a code to exit. Or his lightsaber. Of course, he would have to get by Nil, too.

"Why don't you tell me?" Her gaze was amused as she crossed her arms, tracking his movement. "Which describes me?"

"None of them," he said. "Your ambitions are even grander, I fear."

"You fear? What is wrong with grand ambitions?"

Qui-Gon stopped and faced her again. "You search for the unknowable and attempt to tame what cannot be tamed. Such an effort is doomed to failure."

Only a flare of her nostrils told him that he'd upset her. "So you say," she said, waving a hand. "It doesn't matter. I'm used to being underestimated. You have no idea what I'm capable of."

"On the contrary," Qui-Gon said dryly. "I have a very good idea of how far you will go to get what you want."

"Excellent point," she said, amused again. "You are a worthy adversary, Qui-Gon Jinn."

"I'm hardly an adversary," he responded. "Am I not your subject?"

"I have a feeling you are subject to no one," she answered, the same faint smile on her face.

Nil glanced at her and then gave Qui-Gon a look of pure loathing.

He is jealous, Qui-Gon realized. *Perhaps that is something I can use.*

Zan Arbor might have regretted her softer tone, for she turned away and said briskly, "Now for your part of the deal."

She seated herself at a monitor. "I implanted sensors in your body when I treated your wounds. I am waiting. Use the Force."

"I need strength to use the Force —"

"Stop stalling," she snapped.

Qui-Gon was weak, but he knew he could reach out for the Force and it would be there. He could not show Zan Arbor how much he could depend on it.

He gazed at a clipboard on the table. Using the Force, he caused it to slide rapidly off the table and clatter to the floor.

"A trick a first year student could accomplish!" Jenna Zan Arbor sneered. "I can't get a reading from that!"

Good. "It is the best I can do," Qui-Gon said.

"Liar!" She sprang up from her chair. "How dare you defy me! Don't you realize that you are at my mercy?"

"We made a bargain. You would give me an hour of freedom if I accessed the Force. I did so. I do not think you have the right to be angry," Qui-Gon said steadily.

She moved closer to him. "I . . . rule . . . you," she spat out in his face. "Don't forget that."

She snapped her fingers at Nil. "Put him back in the chamber."

"I see you do not keep your word," Qui-Gon said, as Nil grabbed him.

"Do not play with me, Qui-Gon Jinn," she answered angrily. "I know exactly how much strength you have. You think you can deceive me. I will always be one step ahead of you.

Don't you understand yet how much I know? You barter for your freedom with nothing. So you will get nothing from me."

Only too glad to use brutality against Qui-Gon, Nil roughly pushed him back to the square outline of the chamber. The transparent walls began to rise.

"The amount of effort you use for the Force will result in the amount of time you are given your freedom," Jenna Zan Arbor told him. "Think about it."

The vapor rose around him as the walls surrounded him. Qui-Gon felt despair rise with the enclosing walls.

I need you, Obi-Wan. Find me soon.

CHAPTER 8

Obi-Wan and Astri hitched a ride on a tech transport to Sorrus. The planet was a large one, with varied climates. Over its vast surface were rugged mountain ranges, huge deserts, and sprawling cities. Large bodies of water were scarce, and a complex irrigation system crisscrossed the planet in an intricate series of waterways and pipes.

The pilot of the tech transport landed in Yinn La Hi, one of three capital cities. Obi-Wan thanked him for the lift.

The pilot gazed out at the city. "Good luck to you. I hope you know where you're going."

"A desert region called Arra," Obi-Wan told him, picking up his survival pack. "Are the Sorrusians a friendly people?"

The pilot grinned. "Sure. As long as you don't ask them any questions."

Obi-Wan understood the pilot's words within

a short amount of time. He asked three different passersby for information on where to find transport to Arra. Each Sorrusian ignored him.

"Friendly place," Astri said. "I can see where Reesa On gets her sparkling personality."

Ahead Obi-Wan glimpsed a transport center. There, a clerk behind an information desk directed them to a public air transport that made one stop at an outpost in the desert of Arra.

Although it was customary throughout the galaxy for Jedi to hitch rides on public transport without payment, here on Sorrus there was no such courtesy extended. Astri and Obi-Wan paid for their seats with their few credits.

It was a journey of several hours to the desert. The cities thinned out and the landscape became rugged. They flew over a mountain range. On one side were green fields, on the other desert. Dunes stretched as far as the eyes could see, with not a green plant growing. All Obi-Wan could see were rocks.

The transport pulled up to a desolate landing platform. Obi-Wan and Astri were the only ones to exit.

The air transport rose and disappeared. They stood on the platform and gazed at the sea of sand. The wind blew pellets into their faces, and they pulled up their hoods.

"What now?" Astri asked.

"I have the coordinates of the last-known camp of the tribe," Obi-Wan said. "Let's start walking."

"I'm beginning to worry that this might be a waste of time," Astri said as she trudged beside him. "We might not find the tribe at all."

"It's too soon to worry," Obi-Wan answered. But he, too, felt uncertain. There wasn't a sign of life anywhere, not even vegetation. Who could survive in such a harsh land? Perhaps the tribe had moved on.

They hiked to a sheltered canyon near the foothills of the mountain range. The coordinates matched what Tahl had given him, but there was no sign of a tribe. Obi-Wan slogged through the sand, looking for a clue.

"If they were here, they aren't now," Obi-Wan said. He kicked at a rock. "I don't know how any living being could survive here. There's no food, no water."

"I wouldn't be so sure." Astri bent down and showed him the underside of the rock. It was covered in a greenish substance. She grinned. "Hungry?"

Obi-Wan smiled and turned to scan the walls of the canyon. "I think there might be caves in the canyon wall."

Astri squinted. "Perhaps they take shelter there during the hot part of the day."

"It's worth a look," Obi-Wan agreed.

Suddenly, an eerie, high-pitched sound split the air. Obi-Wan could not tell if it was the wind, or some strange being.

"What was that?" Astri asked fearfully.

He glanced around, searching for movement. His hand went to his lightsaber. He sensed danger, but he did not know where it was located.

The Force whirled around him, pulsating with the rhythm of the moving sand. He saw a flicker of movement high above. Something was flying down toward him from the canyon wall. Then, more and more shapes filled the air.

Not shapes. Sorrusians. Obi-Wan and Astri were under attack!

Obi-Wan leaped backward as one Sorrusian nearly landed on top of him. They were armed with weapons Obi-Wan had never seen before. They were carved from bone and sharpened on each end. His attackers whirled them in a circle so fast that the sharpened ends were just a deadly blur. There were ten, eleven, twelve of them. He was vastly outnumbered.

Unused to battle, Astri stumbled backward, panic on her face at the numbers of Sorrusians. She fumbled for her vibroblade.

Obi-Wan needed to move fast to cover Astri. He leaped and spun, neatly cleaving his opponent's weapon in two.

"Stay behind me, Astri!" he called. She moved

a few steps backward, already slashing with her vibroblade at an attacker from her right.

Obi-Wan cleanly sliced another Sorrusian's weapon in two, and sprang to protect Astri from three Sorrusians advancing from different directions.

Astri's vibroblade came down on the sharp blade of the Sorrusian weapon, slicing it to a dull end. Lightsaber pulsing, Obi-Wan whirled and dispatched two opponents with a sky-to-ground sweep followed by a quick reversal. He dropped to one knee and sliced the weapon of the third.

The others had seen what the lightsaber could do and began to retreat. Obi-Wan saw this with relief. He did not want to harm any members of this tribe. Any chance he had of cooperation would be lost.

One of the robed members of the tribe raised a hand and emitted a harsh, cawing sound. Simultaneously, the rest of the tribe dropped their weapons.

"We do not bring trouble to your people," Obi-Wan said to the Sorrusian who had raised his hand. "We come for help."

"We do not help strangers."

There was a gasp when Obi-Wan deactivated his lightsaber and it disappeared with a buzzing sound.

The Sorrusian leader circled around Obi-Wan and Astri. He said something in a dialect Obi-Wan didn't understand. His gestures indicated that they had hoped to find something worth stealing and were disappointed.

Obi-Wan reached into his survival pack. "I have food capsules." He held out a handful of capsules, and they were quickly snatched away. A female handed them out to the children first.

Obi-Wan watched the tribe eat hungrily. There wasn't much to satisfy them. He wished he had more food. Astri quickly distributed her rations as well.

Obi-Wan took a few steps toward the leader, who had refused the rations and watched the tribe eat.

"Why do you stay here if you are starving?" Obi-Wan asked. "Across the mountains is a fertile valley."

The leader said nothing. Obi-Wan feared the stony Sorrusian silence would not crack. But the leader must have felt he owed Obi-Wan a response since they had given a gift of food.

"You think we remain here because we choose to do so?" He shook his head. "Once there were fertile patches in the desert as well. We planted and had plenty to eat. It was a hard life, but it suited us. Then ten years ago a dam was built. The water was diverted from our lands. Harsh winters have followed, one after another. What little land we were able to cultivate has dried up."

"Then why do you remain?"

"We have tried to move to more fertile lands, but are constantly driven back by other tribes. We are too weak to take land by force."

"The government of Sorrus will not help you? The planet has an irrigation system —"

The leader gave a harsh laugh. "The government of Sorrus built the dam. And worst of all, our tribe voted for it. We were told it would benefit us. But to get irrigation systems, one must bribe officials."

The members of the tribe began to drift back toward the canyon wall.

"We have come looking for someone," Astri said to the leader.

He did not answer, but kept his glance on the sandy expanse.

"She uses the alias Reesa On," Obi-Wan said. "She is a bounty hunter. She is about my companion's height and size, but with a shaved head. You must know her. She comes from your tribe."

The leader did not answer this time.

"Please help us," Astri said quietly. "Lives of those we treasure depend on it."

The leader simply walked away.

Astri looked after him, distress on her face. "Make him tell us, Obi-Wan. We can't just give up."

No, they couldn't give up. But what could they do?

A Sorrusian boy a little younger than Obi-Wan came forward. "I know who you are looking for," he told them. "I know her real name and things about her. I can tell you things."

Obi-Wan gave him a shrewd glance. "What do you want in return?"

The boy pointed to Obi-Wan's lightsaber. "This."

No Jedi was ever willingly separated from his lightsaber. Obi-Wan reached out with the Force. He turned his attention to the boy's mind.

"You admire the lightsaber, but do not want to possess it," Obi-Wan said. "You will tell us the information freely."

The boy looked puzzled. "No, I won't. I just told you that. It's a trade, or nothing."

It never failed to amaze him. Just when he began to feel confident of his Jedi abilities, he was reminded that he was only an apprentice. He could not access the Force as surely as Qui-Gon. He could not affect the boy.

"Come on. What do you say?" The boy's avid eyes rested on Obi-Wan's lightsaber, tucked securely in his belt.

Stricken with doubt, Obi-Wan hesitated. He could not give up his lightsaber. It was unthinkable. But was it the only way to save his Master?

He felt trapped between centuries of Jedi tradition and his own anguish. The dilemma squeezed the air from his lungs. He could not speak. He could not choose.

And meanwhile, his Master could be dying.

CHAPTER 9

The next time she let him out of the tank, Qui-Gon was alarmed at the extent of his relief. He had feared that she would change her mind.

Again, he fell to the floor of the lab. Again, he did not rise until he was sure he would be able to stand.

Dressed once more in white, her pale hair drawn back, she surveyed him with glittering eyes. "I am disappointed in you."

His small smile was an effort. "How tragic for me."

"You are not weakening as fast as the others. I don't know why."

"I am sorry to disappoint you. Should I try to die quicker?"

Nil sidled forward a few more steps, his hostile gaze on Qui-Gon. He poked him with the barrel of a blaster. "Do not joke with Madame!"

"Are you going to help me this time so you

can have your freedom a little longer?" Zan Arbor asked sharply.

"If I'm to help you, I need strength. I must use my muscles," Qui-Gon said. "If I could walk outside the lab . . ."

She shook her head. "Impossible."

"If you want me to use the Force, why do you weaken me?" Qui-Gon asked. "When the body weakens, its ability to connect to the Force does as well."

"I know that," Zan Arbor snapped. She prowled around the lab restlessly. "I discovered that right away. But I need to analyze your blood. I believe there is a way to harness the Force in it. But I can't find it! If I can discover more properties of the Force and how it's used, I can begin to break down exactly what it is."

Qui-Gon did not want to anger her, only distract her. He wanted her to forget how long he was outside the chamber.

"What about your other research?" he asked. "Is investigating the Force worth giving all that up? You saved beings throughout the galaxy. You are renowned."

"I am tired of renown," Jenna Zan Arbor said, as sulky as a child. "What did I get for it?"

"Respect," Qui-Gon answered. "And the knowledge that you have done good for your fellow beings."

"I thought that mattered once," Zan Arbor said bitterly. "It does not. I still had to fight in the Senate for research money. I still had to convince half-brained leaders to run trials of my vaccines. I still had to spend endless hours trying to fund my projects. I should have been working! I am too valuable to have to waste my time."

"That is true," Qui-Gon said. "I did not realize your difficulty." Jenna Zan Arbor was consumed with her own brilliance, he saw. Such beings liked to talk about themselves. If he was careful not to annoy her, he would be able to stay out of the chamber and learn more about her. His only hope for escape lay in understanding his captor.

"No one does," Zan Arbor said, pacing back and forth. "When famine struck Rend 5 and I bio-engineered a new food to feed the entire planet, did I get a reward? When the Tendor Virus struck the entire Caldoni system and my vaccine cured millions, what did I receive in return? Not enough. I learned my lesson."

"What did you learn?" Qui-Gon noticed that Nil was looking at Zan Arbor worshipfully. His attention had drifted from guarding Qui-Gon.

"That I must not depend on the galaxy to recognize my greatness," Zan Arbor said. "I must depend on myself to raise the funds I need. A famine here, a disease there — what does it matter? They will get sick, they will go hungry for a time. Then they will pay for a cure."

"I don't understand," Qui-Gon said.

Zan Arbor did not answer him directly. "There is morality in the galaxy, but I have not seen it," she mused. "I have seen greed and violence and laziness. If you look at it that way, I do them a favor. I thin out populations and the strong survive."

Qui-Gon saw behind the veil of her words to a truth that shocked him. He struggled to conceal his disgust. His voice was calm and even when he asked the next question. "So you introduce a virus into a population so that you can then cure it?"

But Zan Arbor must have picked up something in his tone. "I forgot for a moment about the Jedi morality. You think this is wrong."

"I am trying to understand your reasoning," Qui-Gon said. "You are a brilliant scientist. It's hard to follow the turns of your thoughts."

The answer seemed to please her. "Of course I approached the problem scientifically. I used models. I calculated how many deaths it would take before a population panicked. Then I introduced the virus in a certain amount and waited for it to replicate. When a certain amount of people were killed, the leader would contact me. Then I would pretend to work on the antidote I already had prepared. When they were desperate and ready to open their treasuries to me, I dispensed it. So you see there were no unnecessary deaths."

Zan Arbor's eyes were shining with the pride of accomplishment. Qui-Gon saw that everything she said made absolute sense to her. He realized that she was crazy.

Did that make his situation easier, or more complicated?

"You are greatness!" Nil burst out.

Zan Arbor did not seem to register his praise. "I had to do this, you see," she said to Qui-Gon. "The mystery at the heart of the Force is my greatest research problem. I had to fund that research. If I get to the heart of the Force, I get to the heart of power. I get to the heart of existence itself."

"And when you do that, what next?" Qui-Gon asked.

"I will have all the power I need at last," she said. "Then friends I have left behind will understand that if sacrifices were made . . . I . . . made them for a good reason."

Qui-Gon noticed the slight hesitancy. "Do you mean Uta S'orn?"

"She is my friend. She has stood by me. Supported my work in the Senate. I was grateful, of course." Jenna Zan Arbor looked uncertain for the first time. "But one cannot let gratitude interfere with science."

"So when you discovered that her son was Force-sensitive, you saw a way to further your research," Qui-Gon guessed.

"He said yes right away!" Jenna Zan Arbor cried. "He would do anything for money. He did not realize the commitment he had to make. He was a scientific subject. Surely he should have known there were risks involved . . ."

"But he did not expect to die," Qui-Gon said.

"I did not expect it either," she said quickly. "But what kind of life did he lose? A life of despair. Uta grieved for her son every minute of her life while he was alive. It is no different now."

"So you believe she will understand," Qui-Gon said.

Behind Zan Arbor's coolness, he sensed unrest. "She must. It is logical."

"It will be an interesting conversation, I'm sure," Qui-Gon said neutrally.

"It is time for you to use the Force," she said suddenly, as if she regretted her words. "And this time, I want to see something more than your moving an object a few inches."

Qui-Gon summoned the Force. He closed his eyes and felt it around him, felt it connect him to the living beings here and the world outside —

wherever he was. He gathered it inside his body to help it heal . . .

And he felt an answering call.

Someone else was here. Obi-Wan? Qui-Gon concentrated, drawing the Force around him.

No, not Obi-Wan. Someone else. She was holding someone else here, someone who was Force-sensitive. And whoever it was, he or she was very weak.

He heard beeping and opened his eyes. Zan Arbor sat at the console, leaning forward to study a monitor.

"Excellent," she breathed.

He let the Force slip away. She turned and scowled.

"I am tired," he said.

"Then you won't mind returning to your chamber to rest," she taunted.

Yes, he minded. But not as much as he had before. Someone else was here. Next time she let him out, he would be ready to fight.

CHAPTER 10

Before Obi-Wan could speak or move, Astri stepped forward. "Why do you want his lightsaber?" she asked the boy.

He thrust out his chin. "What difference does it make?"

"What if you want it so you can use it against us?" Astri challenged. "Why should we hand it over then?"

"I don't want to kill you!" the boy protested.

Astri studied him. "But you do want to find food for your family and your tribe. And you think if you had this weapon you could defeat the tribe on the other side of the mountain."

The boy stared greedily at the lightsaber. "I have seen what it can do."

"There are two problems with your plan," Astri said calmly. "The first is that you have to train for years in order to use a lightsaber. Isn't that right, Obi-Wan?"

He nodded. "Even then, you have more to learn."

"So you wouldn't get anywhere," Astri concluded. "Except maybe you'd cut off your own foot. The second thing wrong with your plan is that it won't solve your problem. Maybe if you fought this tribe and won — which is highly unlikely, by the way — you'd get enough food for a week, or a month. But you'd still be starving when the food ran out. You'd have to fight again. And this time the other tribe would be prepared to meet the attack."

The boy stared at her sullenly. "So what? I would still have the lightsaber. I would fight them."

"Still, we aren't about to hand over such a powerful weapon so easily," Astri said. "We'll make you a deal."

Obi-Wan shot her a look. *We?* He hadn't said a word.

Astri ignored him. "If you tell us what you know, I'll cook you and your family a delicious meal. I'll show you where to find food and how to prepare it so you won't ever have to go hungry."

The boy laughed. "You'll show me how to be a cook?"

"I'll show you how to feed your tribe," Astri corrected. "Not for a week, or a month, but always. And if I can't do it, you get my friend's lightsaber."

Obi-Wan shot Astri a look. He hadn't agreed to this. She put a finger to her lips.

The boy looked out over the vast landscape of sand. Not a living, growing thing could be seen. Slowly, he smiled.

"It's a deal."

"Okay," Astri agreed. "Run and get a pack to put food in and we'll begin."

The boy's name was Bhu Cranna. He followed behind them as Astri and Obi-Wan trudged through the sand.

"I hope you know what you're doing," Obi-Wan murmured.

"You stick to lightsabers. I'll stick to food." Astri moved to the shadow of the canyon wall. Where sand met rock, she dug down into the crack. She came up with a small purple mold.

"Looks delicious," Obi-Wan said doubtfully.

Grinning, she handed it to Bhu. "You'll see."

For the next hour, Obi-Wan and Bhu trailed behind Astri, following her instructions as they scraped mold off the bottom of rocks and dug deep underneath the sand to find roots. Astri cut off strips of flesh from a spiny plant and then captured the juice that flowed from its heart. They crawled on their hands and knees through a cave to find mushrooms growing in the cracks of rocks.

Obi-Wan fretted about the delay, but something told him that information about Reesa On was crucial to finding Qui-Gon. He only hoped that Astri's plan would work.

"When I took over the cooking at the café, I had a plan," Astri explained as she pulled the spines out from the fleshy plant she'd sliced into pieces. "Every week I would feature dishes from one world in the galaxy. Luckily, Sorrus was one of those worlds. I chose it because it's so large and so many Sorrusians travel through the galaxy."

"If this is their own food, why doesn't the tribe know how to find this?" Obi-Wan asked, indicating the plants and mushrooms they had gathered.

"Because we were always able to cultivate crops," Bhu volunteered. "It's only recently that we've run completely out of water."

Astri nodded. "In the Tira desert on the other side of Sorrus, they never had a water source, so they live off the desert. I figured that the same kinds of plants must grow here, too. And they do." She held up a gnarled root. "This is called turu root. Tastes pretty awful raw. But if you cook it right, it can be delicious."

Obi-Wan looked doubtfully at the plant. "I can't

believe Didi's and Qui-Gon's lives hang on a root. Can you really make all this taste good?"

"Just watch me."

Astri pounded roots into paste. She spread mushrooms out in the sun to dry. She ground little bits of leaves and roots and combined them into spices. Then she began to roast this and stir that and assemble the various items into a meal.

When the meal was ready, Astri served it to the boy and his family. Bhu turned out to be the son of the tribe leader, Goq Cranna. He was the first to taste the meal, trying each food one at a time and chewing without expression. The boy and his mother waited, looking at him expectantly. Obi-Wan found that he was holding his breath.

"It's good." Pleased, the father turned to Astri. "Where did you find these things?"

"I can show you," Bhu said.

"And I can tell you about more," Astri added. "But now you must tell us about Reesa On."

The leader stood. "Her name is Ona Nobis. Bhu will show us where to go."

Obi-Wan and Astri followed Bhu and Goq Cranna across the dunes. As they walked, Astri said softly to Obi-Wan, "Now, what was that you said about my not being able to cook us out of trouble?"

"I stand corrected."

"We do not speak of Ona Nobis," Goq explained as they caught up to him. He spoke in short bursts, like the rest of the tribe. "Her name is forbidden. For money, she betrayed us. A shameful thing. The government agent spoke to us of the wonders of the dam. We were skeptical. Yet she urged us to listen. She persuaded us. Later we discovered that she and this agent had conspired together. They knew the dam would turn our land into this arid place. The agent owned land across the mountain. He wanted fertile lands. So he received the water. We received the sand."

"What happened to Ona Nobis?" Obi-Wan asked.

"She left before we realized our mistake. We know how she makes her living. Another shame."

"Where are you taking us?" Astri asked.

"My boy found this place," Goq said. "She kept a hideout. Cleverly hidden."

They came to another, smaller canyon. Bhu hesitated when he came to an outcropping of a rock wall.

"When we turn this corner, the wind will be very strong," he warned. He raised his hood and directed them to do the same.

"It is the way the land is formed," Goq said. "It creates a downdraft. This is a place where no one goes."

They turned the corner. Obi-Wan was nearly blown off his feet. Astri staggered, and he reached out a hand to steady her. He pulled her forward. The wind here was terrible. It drove the sand against their skin and in their eyes. They covered most of their faces with their cloaks.

"This way!" Goq shouted. "Stay close!"

Obi-Wan followed on Goq's heels. The closer they got to the far canyon wall, the worse the sandstorm became. He could no longer see Bhu, who was only a few meters ahead.

When he saw Goq drop to his knees he did the same. He motioned to Astri to go ahead of him so he could be sure she would not get lost.

Obi-Wan crawled, following the others. Ahead he saw Astri disappear into a small opening in the rock face. He squeezed himself through.

Immediately, the wind stopped. Obi-Wan wiped his face and tried to shake the sand out of his hair and tunic folds. Bhu lit a glow rod.

"Follow me," he whispered. "In a few meters, we will be able to stand."

Obi-Wan crawled after Astri. She passed through another opening, and he followed.

Immediately the walls widened. He got a sense of air and space around him. He stood cautiously.

Bhu shined the glow rod. Obi-Wan saw a smooth floor and walls, bedding rolled up in a corner, and something covered with a tarp. He quickly reached for his own glow rod.

He lifted the tarp and held his glow rod high to illuminate the boxes.

"Med supplies. Survival rations."

"We took a vote and decided to leave the survival rations intact," Goq told them. "We did not want her to know that we found this place." He gave a short smile. "We were getting close to raiding the food until you came along. Now we do not need to."

"So she doesn't know you've found this place?" Obi-Wan asked.

Bhu shook his head. "We have been very careful. I think she was here recently. One of the survival ration packs is gone."

"Now we will leave you here," Goq said. "We will wait for you in the next canyon. If you follow the canyon wall, you will find us."

Obi-Wan thanked them, and Goq and Bhu left.

"Here's a datapad, Obi-Wan," Astri called excitedly.

Obi-Wan hurried over. He quickly accessed

the file system. To his relief, the files were not coded.

"These are case files," he said, scrolling through. "Clients. Jobs she took on."

"Any hint of where she could be now?" Astri asked.

"Hold on. Let me access the latest file." Obi-Wan clicked a few keys. He read carefully through the information. "This is it," he said excitedly.

Astri crouched down next to him. "What is it?"

"It's the case she's working on now," Obi-Wan said. "I guess her work for Jenna Zan Arbor is over." He pointed at the screen. "She's shadowing the governor of Cinnatar. That's in this system. It's less than a day's travel from here."

"The governor must be her next target," Astri agreed.

"I'll contact the Temple for a Jedi team." Obi-Wan reached for his comlink, but its indicator light was already activated. Tahl was looking for him.

A moment later, Tahl's clear voice came through the comlink. "We've broken Zan Arbor's code at last. The Jedi are extremely concerned. We know that Zan Arbor is conducting experiments on the Force. We fear that she is holding Qui-Gon in order . . . In order to experiment on him." Tahl cleared her throat. "Her first experiment was on a subject with the initials RS."

"Ren S'orn?" Obi-Wan guessed. They had known that Senator S'orn's late son had been mixed up in the mystery of the attack on Didi. They had not known why.

"That is what we believe," Tahl confirmed. "There is a lab notation that further experiments would be done. Yet none were. The notation is dated a few days before Ren S'orn was found dead on Simpla-12."

Obi-Wan swallowed. Ren S'orn's body had been drained of blood. He had been an experimental subject of Jenna Zan Arbor's. But Qui-Gon was so strong, so clever. Surely he would not suffer the same fate.

"You know our fears, Obi-Wan," Tahl said, her voice low.

"Yes."

"I was hoping you had a lead on the bounty hunter. We are discussing how next to proceed."

"I think I do," Obi-Wan said. "We've found out the bounty hunter's real name. It is Ona Nobis. I believe her next job is to assassinate the governor of Cinnatar."

"We will warn him and send a team there to meet you immediately," Tahl said. "Send Astri back here. Contact me when you arrive on Cinnatar."

Tahl shut the communication. Obi-Wan stared at the datapad of Ona Nobis.

"Come on, Obi-Wan," Astri urged. "There's no time to lose. I'm not going back to the Temple. I'm coming with you."

"Wait," Obi-Wan said.

"Don't even try to argue," Astri said, her dark eyes burning. "I'm coming. Hurry. We don't want to miss the last transport back to the city."

He knew he should be hurrying to catch the transport. But something was wrong. Something inside was warning him.

Always listen to doubt. Even in times of great haste, take time to listen. Then trust it.

Qui-Gon's words. Obi-Wan thought about his hesitancy. Something was telling him that Cinnatar was not where he would find answers.

"Obi-Wan!" Astri called in frustration.

"Tell me something, Astri," he said. "The bounty hunter Ona Nobis is clever. Again and again she surprised us. She even outwitted Qui-Gon."

"Yes," Astri said impatiently.

"So why would she choose as an alias a name that we could trace to the place where she was from?"

"Because she didn't know you would trace it," Astri said.

"A part of cleverness is not underestimating the cleverness of your opponent," Obi-Wan said, shaking his head. "She knows the resources of the Temple. Why would she take such a risk?"

Astri took a few steps toward Obi-Wan. "What are you saying? That she *wanted* us to find her?"

"No. She wanted us to find *this*." Obi-Wan gestured at the cave. "And *this*." He pointed to the datapad.

"But it was so hard to find. Bhu stumbled on the cave by accident . . ."

"It was only a matter of time before some member of the tribe found this place," Obi-Wan said. "They wander in search of food and water. She knows this."

He touched the datapad. "What if she wanted to send us on the wrong trail? What if she is still working for Jenna Zan Arbor?"

"You could be right, Obi-Wan," Astri said slowly. "But we need to be sure."

If he made the wrong choice, it could mean Qui-Gon's life. Yet a choice must be made.

Obi-Wan closed his eyes. He filtered out haste and worry. He breathed in his fear of making a wrong choice and let it go. He listened to his instinct. If it was wrong to go to Cinnatar, where was he to go?

After a long moment, he opened his eyes.

"We are going to Simpla-12, where Ren S'orn was found," he told Astri.

CHAPTER 11

The next time Qui-Gon was released from the chamber, Jenna Zan Arbor was not in the lab. Nil pushed him forward roughly. This time, Qui-Gon did not fall. He had gained back some of the strength he had lost. The Force was helping him now, slowly, by degrees. He was learning now to use his captivity to reach out to the Force and let it trickle rather than flow.

Knowing that at least one other being was held here had helped him. It had given him a purpose larger than himself.

"Where is she?" he asked Nil, trying to sound casual.

"None of your business," Nil growled. "Maybe she doesn't want to talk to you anymore."

Qui-Gon gave him a considering glance. "Maybe it's you who doesn't want me to talk to her."

"You mock her," Nil burst out. "You are not her friend. You don't realize her greatness."

"Well, you work with her, Nil. No doubt you see things that I do not. You are the one who is valuable to her," Qui-Gon said.

"That's right!" Nil thumped his chest. "I am the one who protects Jenna! Don't forget that. If you try anything, I will shoot you down. I will not be the one to miss like Ona Nobis!"

Ona Nobis. That must be the bounty hunter.

"Yet if she only has you to talk to, she might get bored," Qui-Gon added.

"She was not bored before you came!" Nil snarled. "I was enough for her."

So Nil was the only guard.

Qui-Gon drew the Force around him. A sensor light began to glow on the console as his vital signs slowed, but Nil did not notice.

"She doesn't need Ona. She doesn't need you. She has me," Nil muttered. "All this talk distracts her."

Qui-Gon intensified his effort. He knew that when the Force was strong, the sensor would make a shrill sound. He needed a split second of distraction, no more.

The piercing sound of the sensor split the silence. Nil turned, startled.

In that moment, Qui-Gon moved, quicker

than the eye could see. He had gathered his strength for just this moment. He twisted Nil's arm behind his back and disarmed him of one blaster before Nil could blink. He tried to remove the other blaster from Nil's belt as Nil twisted. Nil put his hand over Qui-Gon's, squeezing, and the blaster went off. The pulse of blaster fire pinged past Nil's ear. His eyes rolled back in his head, and he fainted.

Qui-Gon dragged Nil to the door. He remembered the tones of the security code and plugged it in. Then he pressed Nil's thumb against the register. The door opened. He dragged Nil back, but as he did a red light suddenly shone on the console and the door began to close. There must have been an extra security precaution he didn't know about.

Qui-Gon threw Nil down and lurched forward. He got his arm inside the door before it closed.

Pain ripped through him, but he did not extract his arm. He maneuvered his body so that his other arm was free. He reached over to the lab table. A long, steel instrument lay on the table, just out of his reach. Concentrating the Force, Qui-Gon caused it to fly into his hand.

Using all his strength, he pushed the door farther open. It opened, centimeter by agonizing centimeter. When the opening was big enough for him to squeeze through, he wedged the steel instrument against the door to hold it. Then he eased through.

He raced down the hallway, every sense alert. He did not want to run into Zan Arbor. Three doors led off the hallway. One to the left, one to the right. One straight ahead. Qui-Gon paused.

He listened with the Force. He sent out as much of his energy as he could. The effort was exhausting.

He felt an answering burst.

Qui-Gon turned right. He accessed the door and found himself in another hallway. Qui-Gon took the first door to his right. To his disappointment, he saw he had merely accessed a storage area. Shelves ran from floor to ceiling and were filled with durasteel containers and medical bins. He glanced at the labels. There were enough antitoxins and medicines here to cure whole worlds . . .

There was a disturbance in the Force. Qui-Gon began to turn, but he felt a pain in his back. His legs went numb. He fell.

"That's enough!" Jenna Zan Arbor barked.

Qui-Gon saw her approach along with Nil. Nil was carrying a harness. He strapped it onto Qui-Gon, who was now paralyzed.

"Drag him back to the lab," Zan Arbor said. "Thank you, Qui-Gon, for that magnificent demonstration of the Force. I will have some readings to analyze now. Thank my stars I can always count on Nil to be outsmarted."

Nil leaned down. Fury twisted his face.

"We should kill him," he said to Jenna Zan Arbor.

"All in good time," she said coolly.

CHAPTER 12

In a galaxy full of notorious planets, Simpla-12 was one of the most notorious of all. Once, it had been rich in minerals, but held little life and no native beings. The planet had been mined and abandoned. Then gradually it became a landing spot for trawlers and a haven for space pirates. A small colony sprang up, and an economy of sorts developed, based on gambling and the sale of black market goods. Violence was common.

There was only one colony on Simpla-12, called, in a burst of optimism, Sim-First. No other colonies had followed. Instead Sim-First had spread like mold over the planet's surface. The outpost was a sprawling, snaking growth of buildings with a maze of narrow walkways made of metal ties sunk into the dirt. Mud oozed from the cracks between the ties. Many of the buildings had fallen into disrepair and had been patched with scrap metal and odd bits of plastoid materials.

Simpla-12's sun was weak. The planet was known for its heavy cloud cover, which made for a constant drizzling rain that dripped from a sky of lead.

"You take me to the nicest places," Astri murmured as they slogged through the mud.

"It's perfect for someone who wants to hide," Obi-Wan said. Was that why his instinct told him to come here? Was Jenna Zan Arbor's secret lab on Simpla-12? When he had contacted Tahl to tell her his destination, he could tell by her tone that she thought he was on the wrong trail. She did not try to stop him, however. She had sounded distracted, as though she was concerned with more important leads. No doubt she was relieved that Obi-Wan and Astri were pursuing what she felt would be a fruitless mission. It would keep them safe and out of trouble.

Obi-Wan had to agree that he was following the slenderest of threads. He tried to call Qui-Gon, reaching out to the Force. He felt nothing. He touched the stone inside his tunic and felt its reassuring warmth. He could not shake the feeling that every step he took brought him closer to his Master.

It did not take them long to discover the names of Ren's associates on Simpla-12. On a world such as this, information could be bought for a few credits. Ren's associates—Cholly, Weez, and Tup—could be found at the 12 Tavern.

They were directed down an even narrower, dirtier lane. The metal ties that formed the walkway were completely covered in mud and garbage. Ahead a sign with the number 12 roughly painted in red swung in the drizzling rain.

They were almost to the building when suddenly a body came flying out of the tavern's front door. With a thump, the body landed face first in the street, sending mud flying. A second body followed, landing with a squeal and a curse.

The first body stirred. "Weez! That's my foot!"

Astri started forward. Obi-Wan put a hand on her arm. "I think we'd better wait."

A third body flew through the air, landing a short distance from the other two.

"Don't be so touchy!" the third being yelled back at the tavern.

A huge Devaronian stepped out onto the front porch of the tavern. Quickly, the three beings scampered backward on their hands and knees. Obi-Wan could not tell their species, but they were all humanoid.

"And don't come back again!" the Devaronian

boomed. He turned and thumped back into the tavern. The door slammed shut behind him.

"That was your fault, Tup," the first being said. He was the tallest of the three, with hair that straggled down his back.

"Was not," Tup said, wiping mud off his round face. "Gibbertz and ham, who knew he had no sense of humor?"

The one called Weez wiped mud out of his eyes. "Most beings don't like having their mothers called Kowakian monkey lizards."

"I thought his mother *was* a Kowakian monkey lizard," Tup said.

The first being, who Obi-Wan assumed was Cholly, stood and tried to wipe the mud off his face with the end of his tunic. He only succeeded in grinding more mud on. "What are we going to do now? We've been thrown out of every tavern in Sim-First."

Obi-Wan walked forward. "Maybe a few credits would get you back inside one of them."

Tup puffed out childish plump cheeks and blew out a short, explosive breath. "Woosh. Great idea, stranger. Thanks for the tip. Only, guess what? We don't *have* any credits."

"Maybe there's a way you can earn some," Astri said.

"You have work?" Weez asked. He stood next

to Cholly. He was a few inches shorter. "Sorry. We have a back injury."

"I can see why, if you keep getting thrown out of places," Astri said.

"The galaxy," Cholly said sadly, "conspires against us."

Tup struggled to his feet. "We are merely victims of its violent tendencies."

"Innocents must suffer," Weez sighed. "Such is fate."

The three stood next to one another. Covered in mud, they were like three descending steps. This ridiculous trio was his best lead to Qui-Gon?

Patience, young Padawan. Suspend your judgment, and every being has something to teach you.

Obi-Wan sighed. "We're not offering you a job. We want information and we're willing to pay for it."

Cholly attempted to look shrewd. "What kind of information? We don't squeal on friends."

"Unless they get on our nerves," Weez said quickly.

"This friend is dead," Obi-Wan said.

"In that case, let's see the credits," Cholly said, as Weez and Tup looked more cheerful.

Astri held out a few credits.

"That's all?" Tup asked in dismay.

"We haven't heard anything worth paying for yet," Obi-Wan pointed out.

"What do you want to know?" Cholly asked. He reached out for the credits, but Astri closed her fist before Cholly could grab the currency.

"It's about Ren S'orn," Obi-Wan said. "Can you tell us about his last days?"

At the name, the three friends traded sad glances.

"Ren." Tup took a deep breath, then let out a long, drawn-out sigh. "Poor Ren. He told us about this offer he got. He was going to get paid a lot of credits. We're always talking about the big score. Something to get us out of here. Ren said he found it."

"Did he say what it was?" Astri asked.

"He was going to be part of this big experiment," Weez said. "Some scientist thought his brain was really special or something. Wanted to study him. Ren said he'd do it for awhile, but she was going to end up paying bigger than she thought."

"Obviously, Ren ended up paying bigger than *he'd* thought," Cholly said. The three friends bowed their heads.

"Did he tell you where the lab was?" Obi-Wan asked.

The three of them shook their heads. "When he got back, he wouldn't say."

"What was he like when he came back?" Astri asked.

"Different," Tup said.

"Weak," Weez said. "He shook all the time."

"He was scared," Cholly said flatly.

"And then he was killed," Tup said. "Woosh. It was sad."

Again, the three bowed their heads.

"Why was he scared?" Astri demanded.

"Don't know. He wouldn't say."

"Maybe Tino would know," Weez said.

"Who's Tino?" Obi-Wan asked. Asking this trio questions was like pulling the fur off a Wookiee one hair at a time.

"Ren's roommate. He took him in when he got back from that experiment," Cholly said.

"Ren said he needed to hide out for awhile," Weez added. "Tino used to hang around with us, but he got a job. Works over in that big warehouse near the landing platform."

"Can we have the credits now?" Cholly asked. He held out a hand.

Astri counted out a few credits.

"Hey, that's not very much," Weez complained.

"You didn't give us very much," Obi-Wan

said. He had a feeling the three knew more. He was anxious to talk to Tino.

Obi-Wan and Astri left the three squabbling about how to divide up the credits and hurried back the way they'd come. Obi-Wan had noticed the big warehouse by the landing platform.

"Maybe Tino will have more answers than that bunch," he told Astri.

"Let's hope so," she agreed.

By the time they reached the warehouse they were almost as muddy as Cholly, Weez, and Tup. Huge loading doors stood open and inside they could see a multilayered structure of catwalks, ladders, ramps, and chutes. Small, compact tech droids rolled through the aisles, pushing gravsleds filled with durasteel crates and boxes. Obi-Wan scanned the area until he glimpsed the person in charge, a woman of middle years in a gray unisuit with a headset, who was barking orders at the droids.

Obi-Wan approached her.

"We're looking for Tino," Obi-Wan said.

She didn't take her eyes off the droids. "He's unloading in Sector Two. Through that door there. Tell him to get a move on and get back here," she said. "I need those droids!"

Obi-Wan and Astri followed the woman's directions and hurried through the door into the Sector One portion of the huge warehouse.

There was no one on the ground floor, but one level up they saw a sandy-haired young man in a unisuit. Droids on the next level were pushing crates onto a chute. The crates slid down and the young man hefted them and loaded them one at a time onto a gravsled.

Obi-Wan glanced around for the ladder that would take them up one level. He paused as he felt a sudden disturbance in the Force.

Quickly, he scanned the warehouse. The droids moved in orderly rows, the crates rolled down. There was no movement on the catwalks above . . .

Then he saw her one level above Tino. At first she was just a shadow. Then she moved, and the shape became Ona Nobis. Dressed all in black, she looked down at Tino. Unaware, the young man below continued to work, sweeping a bin off the chute and loading it onto the gravsled.

She unfurled her whip.

"Watch out!" Obi-Wan shouted.

CHAPTER 13

Tino looked up, startled by Obi-Wan's cry. Obi-Wan was already gathering the Force to make his leap. He landed on the catwalk overhead and teetered back for an instant, trying to get his balance.

Fortunately, Ona Nobis was surprised and her timing was off. The whip flailed uselessly in the air. Obi-Wan had time to note the shock turning to anger on Ona Nobis's face as he raced down the catwalk and onto the chute leading straight toward her.

Astri was already running up the stairs, trying to get to Tino. His lightsaber in his hand, Obi-Wan dodged the boxes that Ona Nobis began throwing down at him. He did not look forward to tangling with the bounty hunter without Qui-Gon by his side.

He reached the next catwalk. The whip flashed above his head. Obi-Wan saw it coming and slashed at it with the lightsaber. The two lasers tangled as the whip wrapped around the blade of his lightsaber.

Below him, Astri pushed Tino behind a stack of durasteel bins. Ona Nobis unfurled her whip once more, releasing Obi-Wan's lightsaber. Immediately, he charged toward her. In a flash, she set the whip to normal mode and snaked it around the railing of the opposite catwalk. Then she used the whip to swing to the other side. Obi-Wan heard the *clang* of her landing on the metal catwalk.

She now had a clear shot at Tino.

"Astri!" Obi-Wan yelled.

Astri looked up and saw Ona Nobis. Her face was white and drawn with fear but she grabbed Tino and pushed him farther behind the bins, making sure he was safe before joining him. Obi-Wan admired her courage as he jumped on top of the catwalk railing and paused before his leap across open space.

For him, the Force was sometimes elusive. He was still learning. But now he could feel it around him, steady and strong. It was almost as though Qui-Gon was with him, joining his strength with Obi-Wan's. He leaped across the gap.

He grabbed the railing of the opposite catwalk, his body slamming against the metal. He had no time to feel the pain. He swung himself up and over and charged.

Ona Nobis's lip curled as she set her whip to laser mode. With the other hand, she drew her blaster. The fire pinged around him as he swung his lightsaber in a wide swath, deflecting the fire. He moved steadily toward her.

Meanwhile, Astri urged Tino onto the gravsled. Kicking aside several bins, she got behind the controls and pushed the gravsled to full power. It zoomed down the catwalk away from Ona Nobis.

Good work, Astri.

Ona Nobis cracked her whip. It tangled with the lightsaber. Obi-Wan twisted his wrist, hoping to flick the whip away. Instead, it curled back and struck again.

Obi-Wan twirled his lightsaber around in a lightning-fast move, corkscrewing around the flexible whip. It wound around his lightsaber in a complex tangle.

With a snarl, Ona Nobis pulled back on the whip, but could not dislodge it. She fired her blaster, but she was off-balance and Obi-Wan was able to turn away to avoid it.

He knew he would not be able to avoid it for long, however. He needed his lightsaber to deflect the fire. Still, he was anxious to deprive his opponent of her most potent weapon. He did not want to let go of the whip.

Use your opponents' strategies against them and you take away their power.

He took a chance and moved closer. She had expected him to pull back, and he drove her farther off balance.

Get your opponents to lose their grace, and they will lose their purpose, Padawan.

Grimly, he advanced farther, pushing against the lightsaber as she stumbled backward, still unwilling to let go of the whip. Her blaster fire pinged harmlessly on the metal catwalk. Her eyes burned with hatred.

He saw now that two of the fingers of her left hand had fused together. No doubt it was as a result of the injury he had inflicted in the battle in the Cascardi Mountains. The hatred and rage she felt was like a thick toxic cloud surrounding them.

He guessed that if he moved quickly, he might be able to release the whip and strike her down before she had a chance to land a blow. He remembered how casually she had shot Didi. And Qui-Gon. He remembered his Master falling back into her ship. He matched her rage and hate with his own.

Do not meet hate with hate. Meet it with purpose.

But what was his purpose? He did not want to take her life, only her freedom. He needed to capture her. Only then would they be able to force her to lead them to Jenna Zan Arbor and Qui-Gon. She would have to make a deal.

Suddenly, he saw Astri behind Ona Nobis. Alone on the gravsled, Astri drove at top speed toward the bounty hunter. They had her between them now.

Ona Nobis heard the noise behind her. She gave one last, enraged look at Obi-Wan. Then she abandoned the struggle for the whip and leaped over the catwalk onto a ramp below. She slid down, her body straight and sleek. The ramp disappeared through the floor below into a lower level.

Obi-Wan leaped after her. He, too, slid down the ramp, bumping down as fast as he could, keeping his lightsaber in the air.

But when he got to the bottom, Ona Nobis was gone. He saw a small door leading outside that the droids used. He could not fit through it, but Sorrusian bones compressed so that they could fit in small spaces. He had lost her.

Furious, Obi-Wan trudged back up the ramp to Sector One. Astri waited on the ground floor with a shaky Tino.

"She's gone," Obi-Wan said.

"At least she left this." Astri held up the whip.

"Who was she?" Tino asked. He shook his head dazedly. "And who are you?"

Quickly, Obi-Wan explained why they were there. "If there's anything you can add about Ren, we would appreciate it," he finished.

"I owe you both my life," Tino said. "Of course I'll tell you what I know."

He wiped his hands on his unisuit. His blue eyes grew cloudy. "Ren was my buddy. He watched my back, and I watched his. When he told me about volunteering for this experiment, I tried to talk him out of it. He wouldn't listen. Nobody listens to anybody. Especially on Simpla-12. Those clowns Cholly, Weez, and Tup thought it was a great idea."

Tino sat down shakily on a durasteel bin. "He came back really spooked. Said he didn't realize what he'd been in for. He talked this scientist into letting him go and promised to come back. But he wasn't going back, he said."

"Did you notice a change in him?" Obi-Wan asked.

"Sure. He lost all his strength," Tino said. "He could hardly squash a bug. That's why he hid at my place. He kept saying . . ." Tino looked at Obi-Wan. "That he'd go to the Jedi for help, as soon as he was strong enough. But first he had to go back to the lab."

"What was he afraid of?" Astri asked.

"Her," Tino said. "Whoever she is. He said he'd stared pure evil in the face."

Obi-Wan felt a chill. This was the person who held his Master.

"Then why did he have to go back?" Obi-Wan asked.

Tino shook his head. "He wouldn't tell me. Maybe because I didn't really believe him. Ren was always such a big mouth. Always talking about his big connections. Said he came from a powerful family."

"He did," Obi-Wan said.

"Yeah. So I heard, after he was dead. But I didn't know then. So when he said he had to get insurance, that this scientist wouldn't dare kill him if he went back, I didn't believe that, either." Tino looked up, his eyes bleak. "And then he died."

"I'm sorry," Astri said quietly.

"Me, too. You know, I told all this to the security force."

"Simpla-12 has a security force?" Obi-Wan asked, surprised. He'd thought it was one of the lawless worlds.

"The Coruscant security police investigated," Tino said. "Some big Bothan . . ."

"Captain Yur T'aug?" Obi-Wan asked.

"That was the guy. He was in charge of investigating the murder. I told him what Ren told me — that if something happened to him, he had left behind a clue, something that would lead them to this scientist and her lab. I told them to ask Cholly, Weez, and Tup. Ren talked to them, too. But he never questioned anybody on Simpla-12. He just shipped Ren's body back to Coruscant, to his mother. I guess they didn't care that much about solving the murder."

Obi-Wan thanked Tino. He and Astri walked slowly from the warehouse.

"What now?" Astri asked.

"I wonder why Captain Yur T'aug didn't follow up on any leads," Obi-Wan said.

"You know him?"

"He investigated Fligh's murder," Obi-Wan said. "He didn't seem very interested in finding that killer, either."

Astri nodded. "I have a feeling we're heading back to Coruscant."

CHAPTER 14

Qui-Gon floated in the chamber. His limbs felt heavy, but the paralyzing dart was wearing off.

Jenna Zan Arbor's face loomed through the vapor outside the chamber. He could just make out the outlines of her face. "Did you really think you could escape?"

"It seemed worth a try," Qui-Gon said.

"I am tired of our game," Zan Arbor said. "You amused me once. I was kind to you. I let you out of the chamber."

"Let us not forget that it was you who imprisoned me in the first place," Qui-Gon said. "It's hard for me to muster up gratitude under these conditions."

She shook her head slowly. "Look at you. You still have your dignity, even when you are at my mercy."

Qui-Gon met her gaze steadily. "I am a Jedi."

She waved her hand, as if this was something that didn't matter.

"You know," Qui-Gon remarked, "there is something strange to me in your attitude. You seem to have great respect for the Force. Yet you do not respect those who are closest to it."

"That isn't true. I respect you, Qui-Gon. Just as I respect a chemical, or the physical properties of a gas. You are a means to an end."

"You will never gain what you seek," Qui-Gon told her. "There is a fatal flaw in your plan."

She smiled. "So you say. And what is that?"

"Understanding the Force takes wisdom —"

"Are you telling me I am not wise?" she asked.

"You have intelligence. Maybe genius. But that is not wisdom."

He had disturbed her. She covered it with a laugh. "I've heard of Jedi mind tricks. You are trying to get me to doubt myself. "That is impossible."

"Here is an example of what I mean," Qui-Gon said. "You do not recognize what truth is, so you call it a trick. That is why you are not wise, Jenna Zan Arbor. Wisdom is something you cannot identify because you cannot measure it with your instruments."

She struggled to maintain her tight smile. "Anything else I am lacking to understand the Force?"

"The most important thing of all," Qui-Gon said. "An open heart."

Her expression tightened. "That is an abstraction. Meaningless. Enough of your games. Enough of you. The final experiments will begin. Thank you for your contributions to science. You will die in the isolation tank. I need your blood."

The vapor grew thick. Jenna Zan Arbor's face disappeared. The syringe entered and pierced his flesh. He watched his blood move down the tube.

Qui-Gon closed his eyes. Now, there were only two things ahead. Two things he must keep in balance, far apart though they might be. He must hope for rescue. And he must prepare for death.

CHAPTER 15

"Captain Yur T'aug is busy," the sergeant said.

"He will see me," Obi-Wan said firmly. "This is a Jedi matter."

The sergeant paused. Coruscant security forces were expected to cooperate with the Jedi, even if they didn't want to.

"I will ask him —"

Pushing past the sergeant, Obi-Wan strode through the door. Captain Yur T'aug sat at a long, polished desk. He was a tall, muscular Bothan, dressed in the security force navy uniform with tall boots polished to a high gleam. He was bent over, staring in a mirror while he clipped his beard. He looked up in surprise as Obi-Wan and Astri walked in.

"I am not to be disturbed!" he shouted.

"Why did you drop the investigation into Ren

S'orn's death?" Obi-Wan demanded. He had no time for preliminaries.

"How dare you question me!" Captain Yur T'aug sprang to his feet and stalked toward Obi-Wan and Astri. He came within centimeters of their faces. "Get out!" he bellowed.

"Not until I get answers," Obi-Wan said, meeting the captain's gaze resolutely. He had learned from Qui-Gon how to meet bullies with calm strength. He did not raise his voice. Still, he felt intimidated by the captain's manner. He was only a boy. Would the captain listen to him?

"I have no answers to give you," Captain Yur T'aug sneered. "I investigated a murder. The killer was not found. The case file was rotated to inactive. Do you know how full our caseload is here?"

"Ren's friend told you that he might have been killed because he had information that someone did not want to get out," Obi-Wan said. "You did not question anyone else. Why is that?" Obi-Wan paused. "The Jedi are making this investigation a priority, Captain Yur T'aug."

"So they send a boy to question me?"

"I represent the Jedi Council. Know that if you oppose us, we will pursue this matter."

Captain Yur T'aug backed up a step. "Always the Jedi stick their noses in my business and I am asked to accept it."

"We are working for the same goal," Obi-Wan pointed out. "Justice. Did Jenna Zan Arbor pay you to drop the investigation?"

A flicker of surprise flared in Captain Yur T'aug's angry gaze. But was it because Obi-Wan had guessed the truth, or because he did not know Jenna Zan Arbor was involved?

"The Jedi Council wishes to know the answer," Obi-Wan said. "We will go through official channels if we must. It would be easier if you would tell me the truth here and now."

Captain Yur T'aug let out a breath, as if he'd made a decision. "It is true I was asked to drop the investigation. But it was the request of Ren S'orn's mother. Uta S'orn is — was — a powerful Senator. And it was her son who had died. Naturally I followed her wishes."

"Why wouldn't Senator S'orn want her son's killer to be found?" Astri asked, baffled.

"You will have to ask her," Captain Yur T'aug said. "I do not know."

The last time Obi-Wan had seen Senator S'orn, he had been ushered into a grand office in the Senate building. She had been dressed in rich ceremonial robes. Since that time, Senator S'orn had resigned.

She lived in a building near the Senate where other Senators from many worlds kept quarters. She opened the door, dressed in a plain linen smock that hung to the floor. She was not wearing the elaborate wrapped headdress of her home world of Belasco. Her dark hair hung loosely down her back.

She did not look happy to see Obi-Wan.

"More questions," she said. "Where's your big friend?"

"I don't know," Obi-Wan said. "That's why I'm here."

She shrugged, then turned and walked into her quarters.

Obi-Wan and Astri followed. Boxes and bins were piled around them, some of them sealed, others half open. She was packing.

"You are leaving?"

"I am returning to Belasco. To do what, I don't know." She gave Obi-Wan a direct look. "Please ask what you came to ask. I am busy."

The Senator had always been direct. He would meet that directness with his own. "Why did you have Captain Yur T'aug drop the investigation into your son's murder?"

"What good would it have done to continue?" Uta S'orn said with a sigh. "He was killed by some lowlife, some criminal on Simpla-12. He associated with them, gambled with them, probably got into an argument. He led a life of squalor. Why investigate it, why drag every sordid detail into the sun? Who knows what Captain Yur T'aug could have found about Ren?" Uta S'orn's expression was tight and strained. "I did not want to know. Don't you understand? I want it all to go away, and you keep bringing it up again."

"But your son might have left a clue behind to help find his killer," Astri said. "He *said* he would leave a clue behind in case he was killed."

"Can't you understand that I don't care?" she said impatiently. She picked up a blanket and began to fold it.

"What if you knew his killer?" Obi-Wan asked.

"Why would I know the dregs of Simpla-12?" she scoffed.

"We believe that Jenna Zan Arbor was involved in your son's death," Obi-Wan told her.

She whipped around to face him. "That is impossible."

"It is true," Obi-Wan said. "We know that Jenna Zan Arbor is conducting experiments on the Force. We know she contacted your son —"

Uta S'orn laughed in disbelief. "You are on the wrong track. Jenna is my friend. I have helped her with her funding, introduced legislation for her, gotten her onto committees, sometimes at personal risk to my career . . . She would never hurt my son. She didn't even know him."

"Did she tell you that she contacted him on Simpla-12?"

Uta S'orn went pale. She knew the Jedi did not lie. "You know this is true?"

Obi-Wan nodded. "Tell me. She knew Ren was Force-sensitive, didn't she?"

"I told her in confidence . . ."

"This was at the beginning of her experiments," Obi-Wan said, thinking. "She probably couldn't get to any Jedi. She was looking for anyone who was Force-sensitive, most likely. Beings no one would miss —" Obi-Wan saw pain constrict Uta S'orn's features. "I am sorry. I know you miss your son. Perhaps she thought you would not."

"I was not in touch with Ren at the time," Uta S'orn said reluctantly. "I told Jenna I had disowned him. I was trying to be strong."

"She offered him money if he would be a subject in an experiment," Obi-Wan said quietly. "He went. When he returned, his friends say he was changed. He was afraid."

Uta S'orn's legs seemed to collapse underneath her. She sat on a chair. Her hands went to her mouth. "Did she . . . hurt him?"

"We are not sure what happened," Obi-Wan said. "Or why he was killed. Do you know where Jenna Zan Arbor's lab is? Not her official lab. But another lab, a secret lab."

Uta S'orn shook her head. "I didn't know she had one."

"We think Ren left a clue behind," Obi-Wan said. "Do you have anything of his?"

She stood and went to the pile of boxes in a corner. She withdrew a small durasteel bin. "This is all he owned. If there's a message here, I haven't found it." She handed it to Obi-Wan. "Take it. And if you find out your suspicions are true, find her."

"I will," Obi-Wan promised.

Quickly, he and Astri hurried outside. The walkways teemed with beings. The area surrounding the Senate was always crowded.

"We need to go through this bin, but we don't have time to get to the Temple," Obi-Wan said. "I don't want to do it in public. Ona Nobis could be anywhere."

"Didi's Café is close, and I still have the key," Astri said. "Follow me."

She led him down an alley and across the square. Now Obi-Wan recognized where he was. They would approach Didi's Café from the back. Astri snaked through several alleys and they came to the back door.

"Good, the landlord hasn't rented it yet," she said, swiping her key card through the lock. The door hissed open.

There was no power to the building, so Astri

opened a shutter a crack to let in enough light to see. They sat at the long kitchen table. Obi-Wan carefully removed the contents of Ren's bin and spread them out on the table.

A utility pouch with one protein food capsule and a small servodriver. A few credits. A vibroshiv. A few crystals. A deck of cards for sabacc. A tunic with empty pockets. A thermal cape, folded neatly.

They were all items carried by the kind of being who owned little and ranged throughout the galaxy. Nothing special. And if there was a message here, he couldn't read it either. Disappointment thudded through him.

Astri slumped in the chair. "It's a dead end."

Obi-Wan felt a presence nearby. Out of the corner of his eye a fleeting shadow flickered. There was someone hovering outside the half-shuttered window. He did not turn and look. Instead, he signaled to Astri with a glance that something was amiss.

"Maybe there is something hidden in the lining of the tunic," he said in a normal voice. "I'll fetch something to slice it open."

"Try the office," Astri said. Under the cover of the table, she withdrew her vibroblade from its holster.

Obi-Wan left the kitchen at a normal pace but raced up the stairs to the private quarters above. He slid open a shutter noiselessly and looked down at the alley. Someone in a long, dusty tunic was peering in the kitchen window. The hood to the tunic was raised. He could not identify the person as Ona Nobis, but he knew such a disguise would be easy for her.

He eased out onto the ledge and paused for a moment, gathering the Force. He would need help if he was to meet this opponent again. Drawing his lightsaber in one smooth movement, he leaped toward the intruder below.

CHAPTER 16

"Noooooooooo!" the intruder cried.

Still in midair, Obi-Wan looked down at the surprised face of Cholly. Out of the corner of his eye, he saw Weez and Tup spring back out of the way.

Obi-Wan twisted his body in midair to avoid landing on Cholly. But a panicked Cholly moved as well, and Obi-Wan half-landed on him. He cushioned the fall with his hands, feeling the shock of the impact up to his armpits.

"Oof! You're a big one," Cholly puffed.

Obi-Wan rolled off and sprang to his feet. He gazed at the three incredulously as Astri burst through the kitchen window, vibroblade in hand. She took in the situation with one swift glance.

"What's going on?" she demanded. "What are the three of you doing here?"

Tup looked at Weez. "Uh. Sightseeing?"

Obi-Wan deactivated his lightsaber but kept it

in his hand. "You are interfering with a Jedi mission," he said sternly. "There are lives at stake. So answer me, now!"

"Gibbertz and ham, everyone is so touchy today," Tup said. He blew out a breath. "Woosh."

"We have just as much right to be here as you do," Cholly said.

"It's a free planet," Weez added. He frowned. "Isn't it?"

Astri brandished her vibroblade menacingly. "It's a big planet. And there's no one around. Haven't you noticed that?"

Cholly scampered backward. "Whoa, whoa, strong lady, okay, okay. We were following you because of Ren's box."

"What about Ren's box?" Obi-Wan asked.

"His personal effects, yes?" Cholly asked. "We requested them from his mother after he . . . left us."

"We said, for sentimental reasons. We were his best friends," Tup added.

"She said no, why should she give what's left of her son to his lowlife lizard friends?" Weez said. "Some people have no generosity."

"So true, wise friend," Cholly agreed sadly. "The universe is so often against us."

Astri rolled her eyes. "Cut the blather. Why do you really want the bin?"

Cholly, Weez, and Tup exchanged glances.

"Ah, if we tell you, you won't cut us out of the deal?" Cholly asked.

Obi-Wan and Astri exchanged a glance. Obi-Wan did not trust the three scoundrels, but they could give them a lead.

"We'll cut you in," Astri said.

Cholly, Weez, and Tup exchanged another glance. Then they all nodded simultaneously.

"The place where Ren was held," Cholly said. "He said the lab had stockpiled medicines. Vaccines, antitoxins, cures for many viruses."

Astri stiffened. "And?"

"Well. We thought, if such a place has such a stockpile, someone somewhere would want to buy it. And someone would have to sell it."

"So why shouldn't the someone be us?" Weez asked.

"But Ren said no," Tup volunteered.

"He, too, wanted to steal the medicines," Cholly said. "But he did not want to sell them. He wanted to turn them over to the Senate, or the Jedi. Some agency that would disperse them honestly. And get this scientist in trouble."

"We had a small disagreement about this," Weez said. "We would help him steal them, but only if we made a profit of some kind."

"So what happened?" Astri demanded. "Did he tell you where the lab was?"

"This disagreement was not resolved," Cholly said. "Instead, Ren was murdered. But he told us he had the location of the lab in a safe place. So if something happened to him, someone would know where to go."

"Then something happened to him," Tup added helpfully.

"And his mother would not release his belongings," Weez said.

"So we had nothing, just like before," Cholly added. "Until you came along. Then we thought, well, if you are on the trail of who killed Ren, perhaps we can find these medicines somehow."

"So we followed you," Weez said. "You see? No harm done. The end!"

"Unless, of course, you wish to steal the medicines as well," Cholly added. "There is great profit here for all."

Astri grabbed Obi-Wan's arm and pulled him away. "Now we know for sure that Zan Arbor didn't destroy the antitoxins she developed. She has them, Obi-Wan! We have to find that lab!"

"I know," Obi-Wan said. "But they don't know where the lab is."

"May I suggest something?" Cholly broke in. "Perhaps if we could look at Ren's effects, we would see something you did not. Because we knew him, you see. We would understand the message that you could not."

"Why would he leave you a message if he didn't want to steal the medicines?" Astri asked angrily.

"Because we are better than nothing," Tup said.

"At least he knew we would try to find the lab," Weez said.

"I hate to say it, but they make sense," Obi-Wan murmured to Astri.

"We might as well see," she agreed.

Beckoning to the trio, Obi-Wan and Astri led them inside the café. Obi-Wan gestured at the items on the table.

"This is what was in the bin," he said.

Cholly picked up various items. "Not much here."

"No datapad?" Weez asked.

Obi-Wan shook his head.

"No big sign that says, LOOK HERE?" Tup asked hopefully.

Weez picked up the sabacc cards and rifled through them. "We played many a game with these."

"Until no one would play with us anymore," Cholly said.

Weez sighed. "They thought we cheated. The galaxy is so unfair to beings like us."

"Did you cheat?" Astri asked.

"Well, yes," Weez admitted. "We marked the cards. We had our coded system. But we didn't bet much. Se we didn't cheat them out of very much."

"We were fair cheaters," Tup said.

"We are so misunderstood," Cholly said sadly.

"Wait a minute," Astri said. "You marked the cards?"

"It's an honest living!" Tup protested.

Astri took the cards from Tup's hands and spread them on the table. "Look at them carefully. Is anything different?"

The three stared down at the cards for a long moment. Then, tentatively, Tup reached out one finger and moved a card away from the pack.

"Look," he said, pointing to the design on the back. "See the mark?"

"Of course," Cholly said. He squinted at the cards.

Cholly moved another card. Then Weez moved a third. One by one, they separated cards from the pack. Then Cholly arranged them in a row.

"These are marked," Cholly said.

"But the marks don't make sense for sabacc," Tup said.

"They correspond to numbers and letters," Weez said.

"I put them in order for you," Cholly added.

"But what does it say?" Astri asked urgently.

"Do you have a durasheet?" Cholly asked. "I can write it out."

Astri scrambled in a drawer for a durasheet. She handed it to Cholly. Consulting the cards, he wrote out:

L 1 Q 2 B U 3 S P 1 2

"What does it mean?" Astri asked, baffled.

Cholly, Tup, and Weez exchanged glances.

"We have no idea," Cholly said.

"It could be an address," Obi-Wan said. He stared at the sequence of numbers and letters. Different worlds were coded on astrogation maps with abbreviations to identify them. But there were thousands of such abbreviations. He would have to run the sequence through an astrogation computer. The possibilities were almost endless. It would take so much time . . .

Look for the obvious first. Use what you know. Then move on.

He heard Qui-Gon's words as clearly as if his Master had spoken in his ear. "It could be," he murmured.

Astri only half-heard him. "What did you say?"

"S P 1 2," Obi-Wan said. "That's the astrogation abbreviation for Simpla-12."

"So it is," Cholly agreed.

"Could Ren have been held on Simpla-12?" Obi-Wan asked them.

"You could hide anything on Simpla-12," Weez said. "But when he left for the lab, Ren told us he was going off-planet."

"Did you actually see him leave?" Obi-Wan asked urgently.

"No," Tup said. "He said good-bye at a café."

"The rest could be an address," Obi-Wan said, staring down at the durasheet. "How is Sim First mapped?"

"By quads and blocks," Weez offered.

"Everything is on level one," Tup said. "There are plans for levels two and three, but no one on Simpla-12 can get organized enough to build."

Obi-Wan pointed to the sequence. "Level One, Quad Two, Block Unit 3," he said.

Astri stared at the letters and numbers. "Are you sure?" she asked doubtfully. "This could mean anything."

"I'm not sure of anything," Obi-Wan admitted. "But I say we return to Simpla-12."

CHAPTER 17

Obi-Wan hailed an air taxi to transport the group to the Temple. As they zoomed through the crowded air lanes, he turned to Cholly, Weez, and Tup.

"I need your help. But we're not going to steal the medicines in order to sell them," he told them. "It would be wrong."

Cholly, Weez, and Tup looked at one another as if this concept was new to them.

"But we helped you," Cholly pointed out, disappointed.

"Why should we keep helping you, if we don't get anything?" Weez asked plaintively.

"This scientist has a bounty hunter working for her named Ona Nobis," Obi-Wan said. "There's a reward for her capture."

"Hey, wait a second," Astri said. "That reward is mine!"

Obi-Wan shot her an impatient look. "You can

share it. We need their help. And we need it now."

Astri's aggrieved look faded. "You're right."

Obi-Wan scrawled a few items on a durasheet and handed it to Cholly, Weez, and Tup. "Once we get to Simpla-12, we need you to find these items as quickly as you can. Then you'll meet us at the address."

Cholly looked at the list, puzzled. "Obviously, you are crazy, my friend." Then he grinned and tucked the durasheet into his tunic. "But perhaps you will make our fortune. So we're with you."

Obi-Wan had called ahead to alert Tahl that they were coming. He saw her erect figure on the landing platform as they docked. She had agreed to supply him with air transport back to Simpla-12.

Astri leaped from the air taxi as soon as it docked.

"My father?"

"The same," Tahl said. "Obi-Wan, who is with you?"

"Some new friends," Obi-Wan explained. He drew Tahl aside and told her what he'd discovered. "I don't know for sure if Zan Arbor's lab is on Simpla-12," he said. "But there's a chance it could be. And there's a good chance that the antitoxin Didi needs is still stored there — along with Qui-Gon."

"A slight chance is better than none," Tahl said thoughtfully. "If you feel strongly that you must pursue this, then you should do so. But if you find that you are right, contact me immediately. If Jenna Zan Arbor knows that someone has found her, she could kill Qui-Gon."

"I know," Obi-Wan said quietly. "But if I could get inside and find Qui-Gon without alerting her, we would have the information we need to send in the Jedi."

"But how could you do this?" Tahl asked. "And are you sure you could get out again?"

He wasn't sure if he could. But it didn't matter. He had to save Qui-Gon and Didi. That was most important. Obi-Wan glanced at Astri. "I have a plan."

"Do not take any impulsive action, Obi-Wan," Tahl warned. "Simpla-12 is not far. I can send several teams to you if they are needed. And make sure there is no surveillance on the building from the outside. Nothing must alert her that you are there."

"I would never endanger Qui-Gon's life," Obi-Wan told her soberly. "But I feel that the longer he remains her captive, the more danger he is in."

"I believe this, too," Tahl said softly. Her comlink signaled, and she frowned. "Now I must go.

Several teams are pursuing important leads. May the Force be with you, Obi-Wan."

Tahl hurried away. Obi-Wan climbed into the transport, where Astri and the others were waiting. He powered up the engines and headed straight for the upper atmosphere. With every second, he felt Qui-Gon's life was dwindling. With all his heart, he begged Qui-Gon silently to hold on.

Quad Two was on the very outskirts of Sim-First. Here, any attempts to keep order or cleanliness were abandoned. Many of the buildings were sealed with durasteel sheeting. An occasional speeder flashed by, but there were no pedestrians on the walkways.

Astri squinted through the drizzle. "I didn't think Sim-First could get any worse," she murmured.

Obi-Wan consulted a handheld nav computer. "Block Unit Three is this way."

As they walked, the neighborhood deteriorated further. Clouds thickened until the day turned as dark as evening. It was easy to stay concealed. The area was all shadow. Many of the glow lights overhead had not been maintained. Occasionally one would send a weak spot of illumination onto the walkway.

Obi-Wan stopped. A short distance away, across the walkway, was a large, windowless building made of shiny black metal. It took up an entire block unit. He pulled Astri back into the shadow of an overhang.

"That's it."

Remembering Tahl's instruction, Obi-Wan left Astri to watch the entrance and skirted around the side of the building. He moved from shadow to shadow, checking for surveillance devices. He climbed onto the roof of a nearby building to inspect the roof below. He could see no evidence of guards. He used his macrobinoculars to study the building from all sides.

He returned to Astri. "Security must be inside. There's a visual monitor by the front door. There's no thumbprint register or retinal scan. That's good. I have a feeling about this, Astri. This must be the lab."

She looked behind them. "Are you sure you can trust Cholly and the others to come through?"

"Don't worry. They'll do anything for credits," Obi-Wan said.

They didn't have long to wait. Before long, they heard footsteps approaching. Cholly, Tup, and Weez hurried down the street, casting apprehensive glances around.

"Woosh, I'm glad we found you," Tup said as

they approached. His round eyes were full of anxiety. "I didn't know Sim-First could be so scary."

"Did you get what I asked?" Obi-Wan inquired.

Cholly unloaded a number of items from his pack. He handed one to Obi-Wan. "Hope it fits."

"It's for Astri," Obi-Wan said as he handed the black visor to her.

Astri fitted it over her head. It obscured her features and gave her a menacing look. "It's fine," she said.

She took it off and shook out her long, curly hair. Next Obi-Wan handed her a pair of high leather boots. Shrugging out of her tunic, she buckled her utility belt tighter around her waist and pulled on the boots.

"One more thing," Obi-Wan said. "I'm sorry, Astri, but —"

She gritted her teeth. "Go ahead."

Using a vibro-razor Cholly handed him, Obi-Wan first trimmed, then carefully shaved off Astri's pretty curls.

"Such a shame," Tup murmured.

Astri's face was set in determined lines. "It's worth it."

When he had finished, Astri fitted the dark visor over her eyes. Her shaved skull gleamed. Obi-Wan handed her Ona Nobis's whip. She coiled it and fastened it to her utility belt. With the extra height of her heeled boots, she resembled the bounty hunter.

"I just hope they don't look too closely," Obi-Wan said. He turned to Cholly, Weez, and Tup. "You stay here. If the real Ona Nobis turns up, do your best to keep her out of the building. She's very fast, very clever."

"It's three against one," Cholly said. "How can we fail?"

"You have surprise in your favor," Obi-Wan said. "I gave you a contact number for Tahl at the Temple. If Astri isn't out again in ten minutes, call Tahl and tell her to send the teams after us."

"We will take care of everything," Weez assured them.

Obi-Wan wasn't so sure, but he hoped that Ona Nobis wouldn't show up at all. He didn't need much time.

He and Astri strode across the walkway to the building entrance.

"What did you mean, if *I* don't come out?" Astri asked him under her breath. "What about you?"

"If we find Qui-Gon and can't release him, you must leave without me," he told her. "Contact Tahl and tell her what happened."

"I can't leave you, Obi-Wan —"

"You have to," he said firmly. "I am your prisoner. Hand me over if you have to, then look for the medicines. Then leave. Promise me. You could be Qui-Gon's last hope."

He couldn't see her eyes behind the helmet, but Astri pressed her lips together grimly. "I promise."

She pressed the button. Obi-Wan noted that her fingers were shaking. What if Ona Nobis was already inside? Once again, Obi-Wan marveled at her courage. Astri accepted her fear and charged ahead.

"You're as good as a Jedi," he told her softly.

He could not see her expression under the visor, but she reached out and briefly squeezed his hand in thanks.

The face of a guard appeared on the screen. Obi-Wan recognized the fine, feathery fur and the triangular eyes of a Quint.

"It's me," Astri said bluntly, pitching her voice low.

"What are you doing here?" the guard asked.

"I have a Jedi prisoner," Astri barked impatiently. "Let me in."

The screen went blank. Obi-Wan felt the seconds tick away. Would they be allowed to enter?

The door hissed open. Obi-Wan saw Astri take a deep breath. Then they walked together into the secret lab.

The door shut behind them. They stood in a narrow hallway with a smooth polished floor. There was one double door ahead of them with a small viewing window. They started toward it.

The door suddenly opened and the same Quint guard who had appeared on the monitor hurried toward them.

"We're busy here, you know," he snapped. "You'll have to bring the prisoner to holding room C yourself."

"I don't take orders from you," Astri snapped back.

"Why isn't the prisoner restrained?" the Quint asked suddenly, his steps slowing. "You always use servo-cuffs with prisoners." His hand went for his blaster.

In another moment, Astri's real identity could be discovered. He had hoped to get farther than this, but at least they were inside. Obi-Wan reached out and unfurled Astri's whip in one smooth gesture. He snapped it overhead, aiming for the Quint guard. It wrapped around his ankle and Obi-Wan pulled back with a jerk. The Quint went down with a howl. Obi-Wan jumped forward and quickly wound the whip around the guard, restraining his arms and legs. Then he dragged him past the double doors into a long hallway. Astri ran ahead and accessed a door, which hissed open, revealing an empty holding room. Obi-Wan dumped him inside.

"We'd better hurry," he said. "No doubt he's supposed to report back. And there are probably more guards."

There were hallways to the left and to the right, and one door at the end of the hallway straight ahead. It was broken and had been left slightly open, its frame bent. Obi-Wan felt the Force surge. His Master was beyond that door.

Obi-Wan motioned to Astri to hang back. Hugging the wall, he moved silently toward the door. He inched over to peer through the opening.

The lab was bright white and filled with equipment. At first he thought no one was there. Then he looked again at a transparent chamber filled with vapor. Through the clouds of gas Obi-Wan clearly saw his Master, imprisoned. Qui-Gon's eyes were closed. He could even be dead.

Obi-Wan wanted to rush into the lab and smash the chamber into a thousand pieces. But he remembered Tahl's warning to be careful. He took a breath and let his anger go. He must concentrate, he must be calm.

He signaled to Astri to follow him and entered.

He approached the transparent chamber. He put his hands on the smooth wall. Qui-Gon floated, his eyes still closed. Obi-Wan felt choked with anguish at the sight. He knew his Master was alive. Yet he felt as though he had witnessed his death.

He didn't think his voice would penetrate the chamber. Obi-Wan spoke his Master's name quietly. "Qui-Gon."

Qui-Gon's eyes opened. He saw Obi-Wan. He smiled. He mouthed the words.

I knew that you would come . . .

Obi-Wan put his hand on his lightsaber.

"Obi-Wan!" Astri hissed. "Someone's coming!"

He hesitated.

"You can't release him yet," Astri whispered. "If anyone knows we are here, we might not be able to get out again."

Obi-Wan looked desperately at Qui-Gon. He had come so far. He had made so many decisions. He did not know what to do now.

Wait, Qui-Gon mouthed. He signaled with a glance that Obi-Wan should hide.

Obi-Wan heard footsteps. He whirled and grabbed Astri's hand. They dove behind a pile of equipment just as the scientist walked in.

CHAPTER 18

Jenna Zan Arbor spoke into a comlink as she walked to her lab table.

"Nil!" she barked. "Nil! Where are you?"

She banged the comlink down on the table. "Probably turned it off again, the brainless fool."

Bending over, she studied the data streaming across the screen. She turned and smiled at Qui-Gon. Then she pressed a button on the console. No doubt this would carry her voice inside the chamber.

"Ah, some Force activity. Thank you. But it won't save you, my friend. I am done with you. But I'll take all your blood before I let you go."

She released the button and picked up the comlink again. "Nil! Bring Ona Nobis to me immediately! Nil! Usually she's in a hurry to get paid." She looked at the comlink in disgust, then threw it down and stalked out of the lab.

As soon as she was gone, Obi-Wan hurried over to Qui-Gon. He knew now that if he let Qui-Gon remain in that chamber, his Master would die. He activated his lightsaber and cut a hole in the chamber. The vapor escaped, and Qui-Gon began to fall. Obi-Wan reached in to help support him. Qui-Gon half fell and Obi-Wan half dragged him to the floor.

"Master," Obi-Wan murmured brokenly. It was shocking to see Qui-Gon so weak. He always counted on his Master's strength.

"You . . . must . . . help me, Padawan," Qui-Gon said, his white lips barely moving. His face was very pale. He held up his hands, palms out. Obi-Wan pressed his own palms against Qui-Gon's.

He felt his Master's power flicker and reach out toward him. The Force moved between them. Obi-Wan gathered it around him. He felt the Force grow with their combined effort, felt it flow from his fingers into Qui-Gon.

After a moment, the cloudiness in Qui-Gon's eyes vanished. "I can walk now," he said.

He rose to his feet. Obi-Wan rose with him.

Qui-Gon glanced at Astri's outfit. "I see you have a new profession."

"Yes," she said with a shaky grin. "Saving you."

"We must hurry," Qui-Gon said. "There is at

least one other prisoner here. I felt a presence. It is Force-sensitive."

"Didi is dying," Astri blurted. "Zan Arbor has withheld the antitoxin that could save him."

"Then that will be our first priority," Qui-Gon told her. "Come. I think I know where to find it."

Qui-Gon did not move as quickly or gracefully as he usually did. But he gathered strength as he went. They quickly jumped through the half-open door and ran down the hallway. Qui-Gon led them to the supply room he had stumbled upon earlier. He accessed the door and they rushed inside.

"Do you know the name of the antitoxin?" Qui-Gon asked, indicating the shelves.

Astri tore off her helmet and scanned the labels. She placed her hand on a shelf. "Here." She removed several vials and filled a pouch on her utility belt with them. She then filled her pockets with as many other vials as she could. Obl-Wan took handfuls of medicines and tucked them in his tunic.

"What now?" Qui-Gon asked. "Do you have a way out?"

Obi-Wan shook his head. "We've tied up one guard. Are there other guards?"

"I don't think so," Qui-Gon said. "She relies on Nil and the security system. Between the three of us we should have no difficulty. Zan

Arbor does not yet know she has been invaded. Our odds are excellent."

The intercom crackled, and they turned to watch the screen. Ona Nobis appeared.

"I have arrived," she said. "Nil, give me access. Nil!"

"It appears our odds have changed," Qui-Gon said.

CHAPTER 19

Qui-Gon looked over at Astri's panicked face. He could not imagine what it had taken for this young woman to come this far. She had cooked and run a café, and now she was facing death on a dangerous mission to save her father.

"Do not worry," he said softly.

"But now Zan Arbor will realize she's been tricked," Astri said. "We'll all be trapped. What should we do?"

"Leave," Qui-Gon said, opening the door. "We'll have to come back for the other prisoner. Zan Arbor will discover that she has been invaded. But she won't know where we are."

They raced down the hallway. Qui-Gon felt the weakness in his legs as he ran. Strength was returning, but he knew he would have trouble if he had to fight the bounty hunter. He wished he had his lightsaber.

Before they turned the corner toward the double doors, Qui-Gon stopped and peered around. Jenna Zan Arbor had left the doors ajar. She had her back to them. Ona Nobis stepped into the building.

"There's been a security breach," Jenna Zan Arbor said breathlessly. "I can't find Nil. I think someone is here, trying to rescue Qui-Gon. Two people, one of them a Jedi. Maybe both of them. You must find them."

"My mission has been completed," Ona Nobis said in a flat tone. "I came for my payment."

"What are you talking about?" Zan Arbor's voice rose. "I'm telling you I'm in trouble!"

"I am telling you it is not my concern," Ona Nobis said in the same emotionless tone. "You sent me after that friend of Ren S'orn on Simpla-12. The Jedi beat me there. That was my last task for you. I have taken on another job. And I have my own plans for that Obi-Wan Kenobi."

"Listen to me," Jenna Zan Arbor spat out. "There are intruders in this lab. You must search the premises and destroy them."

Ona Nobis did not answer. She held out her hand for payment.

"But Obi-Wan Kenobi could be here right now!"

"I will meet him on my terms. Not yours. Not here."

"If you think I'm going to pay you, you are mistaken," Zan Arbor hissed.

Ona Nobis stared at Zan Arbor with a flat, neutral gaze. "If you think you can threaten me, *you* are mistaken. Keep in mind who I am. Do you want to pay me what you owe me, or do you want to die?"

Jenna Zan Arbor seemed to shrink. She was no match for Ona Nobis, and she knew it. She reached inside her robe and withdrew an envelope. She slapped it in the bounty hunter's open palm.

"You will never work for me again," she said furiously.

"How that crushes me," Ona Nobis said coldly. She tucked the envelope into her belt, turned, and left.

The door hissed shut behind her. Qui-Gon quickly herded the others back to the storage room. With any luck, Zan Arbor would hurry back to her lab to try to find Nil. They would use the opportunity to escape.

She walked by them, her face flushed and furious.

"At last," Astri breathed.

They moved out into the hall and accessed

the double door. They were steps away from the entrance when the speaker buzzed. The monitor at the front door suddenly filled with Jenna Zan Arbor's face.

"Greetings to my unwelcome guests, and to Qui-Gon," she said smoothly. "I assume you are on your way to my door to escape. Perhaps you should pause for a moment and consider this. Do you really think I would be so foolish as to rely on one stupid guard and one basic security system to protect what is mine?"

Qui-Gon stopped.

"I did not merely withdraw your blood, Qui-Gon," she continued. "I also injected a device into your system. Not only does it measure your vital signs — by the way, your heart is beating quite rapidly right now — but it also contains a transmitter. If you cross the threshold of this building, that transmitter will set off another. There is another subject in my lab. If you leave, a poison will be released into his system. He will be dead in thirty seconds. You do not know him, but you are close to him. There is a riddle for you. And a choice." She gave a bland smile. "Perhaps you will accept my hospitality for a little while longer."

The screen went black. Obi-Wan turned to Qui-Gon.

"She could be bluffing."

Qui-Gon shook his head. "She is not."

"But you have no real evidence that someone else is here," Obi-Wan said desperately.

"But I know someone is," Qui-Gon said. He turned to Obi-Wan. He saw the desperation and dread in his Padawan's eyes. "You know what you must do, Padawan."

"No," Obi-Wan said, shaking his head violently. "I will not leave you."

"You must." Qui-Gon put his hand on Obi-Wan's arm. "You did well. You released me from the chamber. But I cannot leave this building, and you must bring those medicines back. Didi's life, and other lives, hang in the balance."

"I can go," Astri said. "I will take the antitoxins."

"You have acted bravely, Astri," Qui-Gon told her. "But we cannot let that much responsibility rest with you. Those vaccines and antitoxins must be duplicated. Both of you must go."

"I can't leave you," Obi-Wan repeated, his voice shaking.

"You must, Padawan," Qui-Gon said. "Getting those medicines back to the Temple is a Jedi mission. A Jedi must complete it."

"There is a Jedi team on the way here," Obi-Wan said. "But now that she knows we have found her. She'll fortify this place. She'll devise ways to keep us out . . ."

"She cannot keep the Jedi out," Qui-Gon said firmly. "Give me your comlink."

Obi-Wan handed Qui-Gon his comlink. Then he gave him his lightsaber. It was the greatest gift one Jedi could give another. Qui-Gon placed his hand on the hilt.

"I will keep it safe until you return for it," he said. "Now go."

Astri hurried forward. She pressed the button to access the door. Fresh air rushed in with the scent of coming rain.

Obi-Wan looked back at Qui-Gon. Qui-Gon saw anguish and heartbreak on his Padawan's face. "I will return."

He nodded. "I will be here."

Obi-Wan and Astri left. The door hissed shut behind them. Qui-Gon stood in the doorway, Obi-Wan's lightsaber in his hand. The stale air of the lab soon chased away the fresh scent of rain. He had seen freedom only meters away. Now it was gone.

He turned back toward the lab and his new enemy. And now the game would begin.

Look for

JEDI APPRENTICE

The Dangerous Rescue

Obi-Wan Kenobi heard the door slide shut behind him. The locking system clicked and whirred.

He stopped short as a wave of helplessness overwhelmed him.

"No," he said.

His companion, Astri Oddo, turned. "What is it?"

Obi-Wan faced the closed door with despair. "I can't leave him."

"But he ordered you to go."

Placing his hands against the door, Obi-Wan shook his head. "I can't."

Astri waited a moment. She did not move, but he felt her impatience. Her newly-shaved head gleamed in the faint gray light. A heavy mist fell like rain and gathered in droplets on their skin.

"Obi-Wan, we don't have time," she said. "I have to get to the Temple."

Obi-Wan nodded, but still he could not move.

Astri's father, Didi Oddo, was dying at the Jedi Temple. Astri carried the antitoxin that would save him. Astri had been a chef at her father's café, and she had bravely joined Obi-Wan in his bold plan to break into Jenna Zan Arbor's secret lab.

They had succeeded in only part of their mission. They had retrieved the needed antitoxins. But Obi-Wan's Master, Qui-Gon Jinn, was still inside.

Obi-Wan spun around and gazed quickly down the dark street, searching every shadow. "Where are Cholly, Weez, and Tup? They can arrange transport for you."

"They're not here," Astri said, anger tightening her voice as she scanned the street. "I knew we couldn't trust them."

Obi-Wan dismissed the thought of the three scoundrels. They had agreed to watch for Ona Nobis, the bounty hunter who Astri had impersonated to get inside. They were supposed to warn Obi-Wan and Astri if she arrived, but they had not. As a result, Jenna Zan Arbor had known that intruders were inside, and Qui-Gon had been trapped. Obviously, Cholly, Weez, and Tup had fled.

But they weren't important to Obi-Wan now. Getting Astri back to the Temple was. As was getting himself back into the secret lab so that he could fight side by side with his Master.

"Let me contact Tahl," he said. Astri handed him her comlink. He had already given his own to Qui-Gon, along with his lightsaber.

Jedi Knight Tahl's crisp voice came through a moment later. "I'm here," she said tersely.

Quickly, Obi-Wan outlined the situation. "Jenna Zan Arbor is holding another prisoner who she claims Qui-Gon doesn't know, but who is close to him. What do you think that means?"

"I have an idea," Tahl said. "Go on."

Poison will be released in the prisoner's bloodstream if Qui-Gon leaves the building. He ordered me to leave the lab and conduct Astri back to the Temple. He said that safe passage for the antitoxin was the most important thing. I . . . felt I had to go, Tahl."

"Of course you did," Tahl said. "Qui-Gon was right to order you. But I don't want you to leave Simpla-12."

Obi-Wan felt relief flood through him. He was only a Padawan Learner. He would need the permission of a Jedi Master in order to disobey Qui-Gon, even if his Master was currently a captive.

"What about Didi?" Astri asked urgently.

"Don't worry, Astri. Jedi Master Adi Gallia and her Padawan, Siri, are due to arrive on Simpla-12 at any moment. You should see their ship in a few seconds. The pilot can bring you back to the Temple with the antitoxin. Obi-Wan, you will work with Adi Gallia and Siri to rescue Qui-Gon. We'll start with a small team, but we're sending more Jedi to Simpla-12 in case you need them."

Obi-Wan saw a glint of silver in the leaden sky. "I see their ship. I'll get back to you."

He ended the communication and watched as the small, sleek transport landed in a dirt field nearby. He had worked with Adi and Siri before. Adi was a brilliant and resourceful Jedi with a gift for intuition. Siri was a tough fighter and faced danger without ruffling a hair. The relations between the two Padawans could be bumpy, but he could not ask for a better team to rescue Qui-Gon.

He saw Adi's familiar regal figure stride down the landing ramp. The smaller, blond Siri followed. Adi's sharp gaze scanned the surrounding area, missing nothing. Then she hurried toward Obi-Wan and Astri.

She nodded at Obi-Wan and turned her gaze to Astri. "The transport is waiting. May the Force be with you."

Even at a moment of great urgency, Astri thought of others. She put her hand on Obi-Wan's arm. "I know Qui-Gon will be safe."

"And I know Didi will be well," Obi-Wan told her.

They had been through much together. Astri had no Jedi training, no Force-sensitivity, and could barely manage to hit a target with blaster fire. Yet Obi-Wan had come to admire her many skills. Her fear was obvious but she never failed to charge ahead.

Now she fumbled as she withdrew the vibroblade from her belt. "Here. You might need this."

He took it from her. "Thanks. I'll see you back at the Temple."

Biting her lip, Astri nodded. Then she rushed off, wobbling a bit in the thigh-high boots she had donned to impersonate Ona Nobis.

Siri's hand rested lightly on her lightsaber hilt. Her bright blond hair was combed straight back and tucked behind her ears. Her no-nonsense appearance matched the way she attacked a problem. She did not waste time.

"Tahl contacted us a moment ago," she told Obi-Wan. "Zan Arbor has blocked out all communications from the lab, but Qui-Gon managed to get a last message through to the Temple. Zan Arbor has locked herself in with the other prisoner. If Qui-Gon attempts to come through the door, she will kill the captive. He is searching for another way inside that room."

"Did he see the other prisoner?" Obi-Wan asked.

Siri shook her head.

"We think we know who he is," Adi said. "He is a Jedi Master."

Obi-Wan was startled. "She was able to hold *two* Jedi Masters hostage?" How could such a thing happen?

"Noor R' aya is an elder Jedi," Adi explained. "He does not live at the Temple. He no longer goes on missions, but he chose to live out his remaining days in seclusion and meditation on his home planet. He disappeared several weeks ago, and we've been searching for him."

"We traced his disappearance to the bounty hunter, Ona Nobis," Siri explained. "As soon as we told Tahl this, she told us about Jenna Zan Arbor's involvement. Noor R' aya must be the other being Qui-Gon sensed at the lab."

"Our first problem is getting in," Obi-Wan said. "There are no windows and only one door. Other Jedi teams are on their way, but the more we delay, the more we risk Qui-Gon and Noor R' aya's lives. And Simpla-12 has no security police. It's just us."

"It's not a problem," Adi said serenly. "We have a way in."

The Early Adventures of Obi-Wan Kenobi and Qui-Gon Jinn

STAR WARS

JEDI APPRENTICE